ALFRED HITCHCOCK

and **The Three Investigators** in

The Mystery of the Green Ghost

Text by Robert Arthur

Illustrated by Harry Kane

F

7443

ART

RANDOM HOUSE · NEW YORK

This title was originally cataloged by the Library of Congress as follows:
Arthur, Robert.
Alfred Hitchcock and the three investigators in The mystery of the Green ghost.
Illustrated by Harry Kane.   New York, Random House [1965]
x, 181 p.   illus.   22 cm.   (Alfred Hitchcock mystery series, 4)
I. Title.   II. Title: The mystery of the Green ghost.   (Series)
PZ7.A744Ah   65 — 22216
ISBN: 0-394-81228-X   ISBN: 0-394-91228-4 (lib. ed.)

The Three Investigators in

The Mystery of
the Green Ghost

Contents

Warning to the Reader!

I do not want to alarm anyone, but I feel it is my duty to warn you that in the pages ahead you will meet, as the title of this book suggests, a green ghost. In addition to the ghost you will encounter some strange pearls, and a little dog who plays no part in the story because he does nothing at all. Or does he play a part? Sometimes doing nothing is as important as doing something. It will be worth thinking about.

I could tell you of many other strange episodes, exciting adventures and suspenseful situations that you will be encountering, but I feel sure you would rather read about these for yourself. So I will content myself by introducing, as I promised them I would, The Three Investigators.

This is the fourth time I have introduced them, and I

admit that in the earlier cases I had grave doubts. However, I have now grown rather fond of Jupiter Jones, Bob Andrews and Pete Crenshaw. I think you will find them good companions for an evening of mystery, adventure and suspense.

The three boys have formed the firm of The Three Investigators and use their spare time to solve any mysteries that come their way. They live in Rocky Beach, California, a town on the shore of the Pacific Ocean some miles from Hollywood. Bob and Pete live with their parents and Jupiter lives with his uncle, Titus Jones, and aunt, Mathilda Jones, who own and operate The Jones Salvage Yard, a rather fabulous junkyard where one can find almost anything.

In this junkyard is a 30-foot mobile home trailer, that was damaged in an accident, which Titus Jones was never able to sell. He allowed Jupiter and his friends to use it, and they have rebuilt it as a modern Headquarters for an investigation firm. It has a small laboratory, a dark room, and an office with desk, typewriter, telephone, tape recorder, and many books of reference. All equipment was rebuilt by Jupiter and the others from junk that came into the salvage yard.

Jupiter has had Hans and Konrad, the big, blond Bavarian brothers who are the yard helpers, arrange stacks of junk all around the trailer so that it is invisible to the outside world. The adults have forgotten about it. Only The Three Investigators know of its existence, and they keep the secret by using hidden entrances into Headquarters.

The entrance they use most often is Tunnel Two, a length of corrugated iron pipe which runs from their outdoor workshop partly underground, beneath some junk and under Headquarters. After crawling through it, they emerge into Headquarters through a trap door. There are other entrances, but we will discuss them when we come to them.

The boys have the use of a gold-plated Rolls Royce automobile, complete with chauffeur, when they need to travel long distances. The use of this automobile, for thirty days, was won in a contest by Jupiter Jones. For ordinary purposes of local travel, they use their bicycles, or sometimes get Hans or Konrad to drive them in one of the salvage yard trucks.

Jupiter Jones is stocky, muscular, and a bit roly-poly. Some people of an unfriendly nature call him fat. He has a round face which often looks stupid. This is misleading. Behind it is a very sharp intelligence. Jupiter has an excellent mind, and he is rather proud of it. He has many good features, but undue modesty is not one of them.

Pete Crenshaw, tall, brown hair, muscular, is capable of many athletic feats. He is Jupiter's right-hand man at trailing suspects and other dangerous activities.

Bob Andrews is slighter of build, has lighter hair, and is more studious. Though he has great nerve, he is chiefly in charge of records and research for the firm. He has a part-time job at the local library, and this enables him to hunt up much information that is helpful in the firm's investigations.

I have told you all this, so that the following narrative need not be interrupted to repeat information which some of you may have previously acquired, if you have read about the firm's earlier cases.

In any event, onward! The green ghost is about to scream!

ALFRED HITCHCOCK

The Three Investigators in

The Mystery of
the Green Ghost

CHAPTER 1

The Green Ghost Screams

The scream took Bob Andrews and Pete Crenshaw by surprise.

Standing in a driveway overgrown with weeds, they were studying an old, empty house, as big as a hotel, one end torn down where the wreckers had begun on it. Moonlight made everything misty and unreal.

Bob, with a portable tape recorder slung around his neck, was talking into it, describing the scene. He interrupted himself to turn to Pete and say:

"A lot of people think that house is haunted, Pete. It's too bad we didn't think of it when Alfred Hitchcock was looking for a haunted house for one of his pictures." He was referring to the time they had become acquainted with the famous movie director when they had solved the

3

mysterious secret of Terror Castle.

"I bet Mr. Hitchcock would have liked this place, all right," Pete agreed. "But I don't. In fact, every minute I'm getting more nervous. "What do you say we get away from here?"

That was when the scream came from the house.

"EEEeeeee-*aahhhhhh!*" It was a high-pitched sound, almost more animal than human. The hair stood up on both boys' necks.

"Did you hear that?" Pete gulped. "Now we *are* getting out of here!"

"Wait!" Bob said, standing his ground despite an impulse to run. As Pete hesitated he said, "I'll turn up the tape recorder in case we hear anything else. That's what Jupiter would do."

He was referring to Jupiter Jones, their partner in the firm of The Three Investigators, who was not with them.

"Well——" Pete began. But Bob had already turned up the volume control and pointed the microphone at the empty, mouldering old house among the trees.

"Aaaaaaahhhhh—ahheeeee—*eeeeee!*" The scream came again and died out slowly, in a most unsettling manner.

"Now let's go!" Pete said. "We've heard enough!"

Bob was in full agreement. They spun around and started to run down the old driveway to where their bikes were parked.

Pete was fleet as a deer, and Bob ran faster than he had

run for many years. After a fall down a rocky slope, he had broken his leg in several places and for a long time he had had to wear a brace. However, the leg had healed well, and after a long period of exercises, Bob was told, just the previous week, that he could discard the brace.

Now, without it, he felt so light he could almost fly. But fast as they ran, neither he nor Pete got very far.

Strong arms suddenly and unexpectedly stopped them.

"Ah-ulp!" Pete grunted in surprise as he ran headlong into someone behind him. Bob, too, was brought up short by plunging into a man who grabbed him and held him.

They had run full tilt into a group of men who had come up the driveway behind them as they stood listening to the eerie screams.

"Whoa, boy!" the man who had grabbed Pete exclaimed good-naturedly. "You nearly knocked me down!"

"What was that sound?" asked the man who had caught Bob from falling as the boy ran blindly into him. "We saw you boys standing and listening."

"We don't know what it was," Pete spoke up. "But it sounded like the ghost to us!"

"Ghost, nonsense! . . . It could be someone in trouble! . . . Maybe it was just a tramp. . . ."

The five or six men in the group into which the boys had plunged all began to speak at once, ignoring Pete and Bob now. The two boys could not see their faces clearly. But they all seemed well-dressed and spoke like typical dwellers in the pleasant neighborhood that surrounded the overgrown grounds and the empty house, known as the Green estate.

"I think we should go inside!" One man with an unusually deep voice spoke loudly. Bob couldn't make out his features, except to see that he had a moustache. "We came over here to look at the old building before it got torn down. We heard somebody scream. Somebody may be inside, hurt."

"I say we should call the police," said a man in a checked sports jacket, a little nervously. "It's their duty to investigate such things."

"Someone may be hurt," the deep-voiced man said. "Let's see if we can help. If we wait for the police he might die."

"I agree," spoke up a man wearing thick glasses. "I think we should go inside, and look around."

"You can go inside, I'll go get the police," said the man in the checked coat. He had turned away when a man who led a small dog on a leash spoke up.

"It may be just an owl or a cat that's gotten inside," he said. "If you call the police for that, you'll look pretty foolish."

The man in the checked coat hesitated.

"Well——" he began. At that point a large man, the biggest in the group, took the lead.

"Come on," he said. "There's half a dozen of us and we have several flashlights. I say we look inside first, and then call the police if it's necessary. You two boys—you can go

6

on home, you're not needed here."

He strode up the flagstone path that led toward the house, and after a moment's hesitation, the others followed him. The man who was leading the small dog picked it up and carried it, and the man in the checked coat, somewhat reluctantly, brought up the rear of the group.

"Come on," Pete said to Bob. "Like he said, they don't need us. Let's go home."

"And not find out what made that noise?" Bob asked. "Think what Jupe would say. We'd never hear the end of it. We're supposed to be investigators. Anyway, there's nothing to be scared about now, there're so many of us."

He hurried up the path after the men, and Pete followed him. Outside the big front door, the men were milling around uncertainly. Then the big man in the lead tried the door. It opened, showing a black cavern of hallway inside.

"Use your flashlights," he said. "I want to find out what it was we heard."

With his own flashlight on, he led the way inside. The others crowded close at his heels, and three more flashlights cut bright paths into the darkness. As the men entered, Pete and Bob quietly slipped inside behind them.

They found themselves in a big reception hall. The men who had flashlights shone the beams around, and they could all see that the walls were covered with what had once been cream-colored silk tapestries, with Oriental scenes on them.

An impressive flight of stairs curved down into the hall. One of the men shone his light on it.

"That must be where old Mathias Green feel down and broke his neck fifty years ago," he said. "Smell the air! This place has been shut up for the whole fifty years."

"The house is supposed to be haunted," someone else said. "And I'm willing to believe it. I only hope we don't see the ghost."

"We're not getting very far with our search," said the big man. "Let's start by searching the ground floor."

Staying in a group, the men began to go through the big rooms on the ground floor. The rooms were empty of furniture. Dust lay everywhere. One wing of the building had no back wall. That was where the wreckers had started to tear the building down just that day.

The group found nothing but echoing, empty rooms through which they walked hesitantly, talking in hushed whispers. They tried the other wing of the mansion. Finally they came into what must once have been a big parlor. There was an impressive fireplace at one end and tall windows at the other. The men gathered in front of the fireplace, uneasily.

"We're not doing any good," one man said in a low voice. "We should call the police——"

"Sssh!" another voice cut him off. Everyone froze into silence. "I thought I heard something," the second man said in a low whisper. "It may be just an animal. Let's turn off all the lights and see if anything moves."

All the lights winked out. Darkness engulfed the room, except for some very faint moonlight coming through the dirty windows.

Then someone said in a gasping tone, "Look! Over by the door!"

They all turned. And they all saw it.

A greenish figure was standing by the door through which they had entered. It seemed to glow slightly, as if with an inner light, and to waver a bit as though it were insubstantial mist. But as Bob stared at it, unconsciously holding his breath, it seemed to him to be the figure of a man in long, flowing green robes.

"The ghost!" a rather weak voice gulped. "Old Mathias Green!"

"All lights on!" the big man said sharply. "Shine them that way!"

But before the lights went on, the greenish misty figure seemed to glide along the wall and dart out through the open door. It vanished as three flashlights beamed light toward it.

"I wish I was someplace else," Pete whispered into Bob's ear. "Beginning about an hour ago."

"It may have been a flash from an auto headlight," a man said firmly. "Just coming in a window. Come on, let's have a look in the hall."

They all trooped noisily out into the hall and flashed their lights around again. There was nothing to be seen. Then someone suggested that they turn the lights out once

more. They waited in silence and darkness again; the small dog one man carried in his arms whimpered slightly.

This time Pete spotted the figure. The others were looking around them, but he happened to glance up the stairs and there, on the landing, was the greenish figure.

"There it is!" he shouted. "On the stairs."

They all turned. They all saw the figure move from the landing and glide up toward the second floor.

"Come on!" shouted the big man. "It's someone pulling a gag on us. Follow him and catch him!"

He led the way pell-mell up the stairs. But when they got to the second floor, they found nothing.

"I have an idea." It was Bob who spoke. He was asking himself what Jupiter Jones would have done if he had been there, and he thought he knew.

"If anybody came upstairs ahead of us," he said, as the men turned to him and someone shone a light on his face so that he had to squint, "they'd leave tracks on the dusty floor. If they left tracks, we can follow them."

"The boy's right," the man with the dog exclaimed. "You fellows, shine your lights here on the floor of the hall, where none of us has walked yet."

Three flashlights glowed on the floor. There was dust, all right, plenty of it, but nothing had disturbed it.

"Nobody's been up here!" The speaker sounded baffled. "So what did we see go up these stairs?"

Nobody answered that, although everyone knew what everyone else was thinking.

11

"Let's turn out the lights and see if we see it again," a voice suggested.

"Let's get out of here," someone else said, but there was a chorus of agreement with the first speaker. After all, there were eight or nine of them—counting Pete and Bob —and nobody wanted to admit to being scared.

In the darkness at the head of the stairs, they waited.

Pete and Bob were staring down the hall when someone whispered sharply.

"To the left!" he said. "Halfway down the hall."

They spun around. A green glow, so faint it could hardly be seen, stood beside a doorway. The figure grew clearer. Definitely now it was a human-shaped figure in green flowing robes like a Mandarin's.

"Let's not scare it," somebody said in a low voice. "See what it does."

They all waited silently.

The ghostly figure began to move. It glided down the hall close to the wall, to the very end. Then it turned the corner, or seemed to, and vanished.

"Follow it, slowly this time," someone murmured. "It's not trying to get away."

Bob spoke up again. "See if there are any footprints now, before we go down the hall," he suggested.

Two flashlights winked on and played up and down the hallway.

"No footprints!" The deep-voiced speaker sounded a bit hollow. "Not a trace of a print in the dust. Whatever it is, it's floating on air."

"We've come this far, we have to go on," someone else said firmly. "I'll lead the way."

The speaker, the big man, strode out boldly down the hall. The others followed. They came to a cross corridor, where the green figure had turned, and stopped. Someone shone a light down the other hallway. Two open doors showed in its beam. Beyond the doors the hallway ended in a blank wall.

They shut off the lights and waited. In a moment the green, ghostly figure glided out of one of the open doors, down the hall, hugging the wall, and stopped at the blank wall where the hall ended. Then, very slowly, it faded out.

As if, Bob said later, it had oozed right through the wall.

And there were no footprints in the dust.

Nor, when the police came later after the men had called them, could Chief Reynolds or any of his men find a thing. There was no trace of a human being in the house, no one hurt, no animal. Nothing.

Being a policeman, Chief Reynolds did not like to believe that eight reliable witnesses had seen a ghost, or heard a ghost scream. But he had no choice.

Because later that night a watchman reported that he had seen a greenish, ghostly figure lurking near the rear entrance of a big warehouse. It had faded away when he approached. Still later, a woman phoned to the police in a panic, saying a moaning noise had awakened her and she had seen a greenish figure standing out on her patio. It had vanished when she turned the light on. Two truckers at an all-night restaurant said they saw a ghostly figure beside their truck.

But finally, Chief Reynolds had a call from two radio patrol car officers who said they had seen a figure in Rocky Beach's Green Hills Cemetery. Reynolds hurried down there and stepped inside the big iron gate of the cemetery. Standing against a tall white monument was a green, ghostly figure that, as he approached it, sank into the ground and was gone.

The chief flashed his light on the monument.

It was the monument to the unfortunate Mathias Green, who had fallen down his stairs and broken his neck fifty years before in the great, old mansion.

CHAPTER 2

Summons for Bob and Pete

"AAAhhhhhhh---*eeeeeeee!*" The ghostly scream sounded again. But this time it did not bother Bob and Pete. It was coming from the tape recorder.

The Three Investigators were in their concealed, mobile-home Headquarters in The Jones Salvage Yard, and Jupiter Jones was listening intently to the tape that Bob had recorded the previous evening.

"There're no more screams, Jupe," Bob said. "The rest is just conversation when those men met us, before I remembered the machine was running, I shut it off when we went in the house."

Jupiter, however, listened to everything. The voices of the men who had spoken the previous night were quite clear, for Bob had had the recording volume all the way

15

up. When the tape ended, he shut it off, pinching his lower lip, a sign his mental machinery was spinning.

"That sounded to me like a human scream," he said. "It sounded like somebody screaming as he fell down a flight of stairs, and at the end dying out because he didn't have strength enough to scream any more."

"That's just what it does sound like!" Bob exclaimed. "And that's what happened in that house fifty years ago. Old Mathias Green, the owner, fell down the stairs and broke his neck. He probably screamed as he fell!"

"Now wait a minute, wait a minute!" Pete objected. "Why should we hear him screaming fifty years later?"

"Perhaps," Jupiter said solemnly, "the scream was a supernatural echo of a scream first uttered fifty years ago."

"Don't say things like that!" Pete objected. "I don't like to hear them. How could we hear a fifty-year old echo?"

"I don't know," Jupiter answered. "Bob, you are in charge of records and research for the firm. Please give me a detailed account of what happened and what you have learned of the history of the Green mansion."

Bob drew in a deep breath.

"Well," he began, "Pete and I rode over last night to look at the place when we heard they were starting to tear it down. I thought I could do a good story on it and have it ready for the first issue of the school paper in the fall. I took along the tape recorder so I could talk my impressions into it, to use later for the writing.

"We'd been there about five minutes, and the old house

16

was looking mighty spooky, when the moon came up. Then came the scream. The first one. I turned up the volume of the recorder in case there was another scream because I knew it would be important for you to hear it."

"Very good," Jupiter said. "You are thinking like a detective. I've already heard on the tape what the men said. Proceed with your entry into the house."

Bob described in detail how they had searched the house, how they had seen the ghostly green figure first downstairs, then on the landing, then upstairs, and then how it had finally glided down the hall and melted through a solid wall.

"And no footprints," Pete said. "Bob thought of that, and he made sure the men with flashlights examined the floor carefully."

"Excellent work," Jupiter said. "How many men saw this green apparition with you?"

"Six," Pete told him.

"Seven," Bob contradicted him.

They looked at each other. Pete spoke first.

"Six," he said. "I'm positive. The big man who led us, the fellow with the deep voice, the man with the little dog, a man who wore glasses, and two others I didn't notice much."

"Maybe you're right," Bob admitted, unsure of himself. "I counted them inside, when they were all moving around. Once I got six and twice I got seven."

"It probably doesn't matter," Jupiter said, forgetting for

17

a moment his own rule that in any mystery the smallest fact might be very important. "Now give me the background of the old house."

"Well," Bob said, "we left the house and the men broke up into groups. One group said they'd call the police. This morning the papers were full of the story. I stopped at the library on the way over here, but they don't have any information about the Green mansion because it was built so long ago—before Rocky Beach was even a town or had a library.

"But according to the story in the papers, it was built way back, sixty or seventy years ago, by old Mathias Green. He was a skipper in the China trade, and supposed to be a very tough man. Not too much is known about him, but it seems he got into some kind of trouble when he was in China and had to leave in a hurry. He came back here with a beautiful Chinese princess for a bride. One story says he quarreled with his only relative, a sister-in-law up in San Francisco, and came down here to live.

"Another story says he feared the vengeance of some Chinese nobles, maybe the family of his wife, and he built his big house down here to hide. This region was pretty wild back then, you know.

"Anyway, he lived in style in the Green mansion with a whole bunch of Oriental servants. He liked to put on green robes like a Manchu noble. He used to have his supplies brought up to him by team and wagon from down in Los Angeles, once a week, and one day the driver of the wagon found the house empty. Except for Mathias Green. He lay at the bottom of the stairs with his neck broken.

"When the police finally got there, they decided that he had been drinking and had fallen down and killed himself and that the whole bunch of servants had fled in the night, afraid they'd be blamed. Even the Chinese wife was gone.

"They could never find anybody to tell them anything. In those days most Chinese in this country were very secretive and afraid of the law, so all the servants either went back to China or went up to San Francisco and lost themselves in Chinatown, there.

"Anyway, the whole thing stayed a mystery. His widowed sister-in-law in San Francisco inherited his estate, and used the money he left her to buy a vineyard up in Verdant Valley, near San Francisco. She refused to live in the house or to sell it either. Even after she died, it was just left here to rot. Finally, though, this year a Miss Lydia Green, the sister-in-law's daughter, sold the property to a developer who is going to tear down the house and build some modern houses on the grounds.

"That's why the house was being torn down. And— well, that's about all I can tell you."

"Very well summed up, Records," Jupiter complimented Bob. "Now let us examine the newspaper accounts."

He spread out several newspapers on the desk of the tiny Headquarters office. There was a Los Angeles paper, a San Francisco paper and the local paper. The local paper had the biggest headlines about the strange events

19

of the night before, but the big city papers gave it plenty of space, too, with dramatic headlines such as:

**SCREAMING GHOST LEAVES
WRECKED HOME TO BRING
TERROR TO ROCKY BEACH.**

**GREEN GHOST AT LARGE
IN ROCKY BEACH AS
HOME IS TORN DOWN.**

**GREEN GHOST LEAVES
WRECKED HOME TO
SEEK NEW LODGINGS**

The stories that followed were written in a humorous vein, but they gave the facts as Bob had just stated them. Missing was the fact that Police Chief Reynolds and two of his men had actually seen the green figure in the cemetary. He preferred to keep that to himself. He didn't want to be made a laughing stock.

"The paper says," Jupiter remarked, referring to the *Rocky Beach News*, "that the ghost was seen outside a big warehouse, then later in a woman's patio, and finally among some big trucks outside a truckmen's diner. It almost looks as if the ghost was looking for someplace else to stay, now that his home is being torn down."

"Yeah," Pete said with a note of sarcasm. "Maybe he was hitchhiking away from Rocky Beach."

"Perhaps." Jupiter chose to take the remark seriously. "Although ghosts are not commonly supposed to need mundane means of transportation."

"Long words," Pete groaned. He put his head down on his arms as if floored by Jupiter's language. "Long words Jones! You know I don't know what mundane means."

"It means ordinary or everyday," Jupiter told him. "The whole thing seems very mysterious. Until further facts emerge——"

He was interrupted by his aunt's voice. Mrs. Mathilda Jones was a large woman, and her voice was a powerful one. It was she who really ran The Jones Salvage Yard, the family business.

"Bob Andrews!" the boys heard her calling. "Come out from behind all that junk and show yourself. Your father is here and wants you. Pete, too."

CHAPTER 3

The Hidden Room

In a moment all three boys were scrambling through the long section of corrugated pipe which formed Tunnel Two, the secret entrance they used most. They had put some old carpets on the bottom, so that the corrugations didn't bruise their knees, and they could slither out through the exit as fast as eels. In a moment they were threading their way through the stacks of junk which Jupiter had had Hans and Konrad, the yard helpers, arrange to hide their workshop and Headquarters. They emerged in the open space around the neat shack which served as the office for the salvage yard.

There Mathilda Jones waited, talking with Bob's father, a tall man with twinkling eyes and a brown moustache.

"There you are, son!" he said. "Come along, we have to

hurry. Chief Reynolds wants to talk to you. You, too, Pete."

Pete gulped. Chief Reynolds wanted to talk to him? He thought he knew what about—the events of the previous night.

Jupiter's round features looked eager. "May I go, too, Mr. Andrews?" he asked. "After all, we're a team. All three of us."

"I guess one more boy won't matter." Mr. Andrews smiled. "But come along. Chief Reynolds is outside in a police car and we're going to ride with him."

Just outside the gate a black sedan was waiting. Police Chief Reynolds, a bulky man, a bit bald, was at the wheel. His mouth and chin looked grim.

"Good work, Bill," he said to Bob's father. "Now let's get there fast. And listen—you're a local man—we're neighbors. I'm counting on you to help me handle the outside press if this thing—well, if this crazy business turns into something even crazier.

"You can count on me, Chief," Mr. Andrews said. "While we drive over to the Green mansion, why don't you let my son tell you what he and his friend observed last night."

"Yeah, shoot, boy," Chief Reynolds said, starting the car down the road at breakneck speed. "I've heard it from a couple of the men who were there, but let's hear how you saw it."

Bob swiftly told him what he and Pete had observed the

previous evening. Chief Reynolds chewed his lips as he listened.

"Yes, that sounds just about like what the others told me," he said gloomily. "Even with so many witnesses I'd say it was impossible only—"

He stopped. Bob's father, who was a very good reporter, looked at him sharply.

"Something tells me, Sam," he said, "that you saw that green ghost yourself. That's why you aren't speaking up louder to say that it is impossible."

"Yes." The chief let out a gusty sigh. "I saw it, too. At the cemetery. Standing by the marble shaft erected to old Mathias Green. And, confound it, as I watched it, that green figure just sank down into the ground where the grave is and vanished!"

Pete, Bob and Jupiter were sitting on the edge of the seat, listening with great excitement. Bob's father looked quizzically at the chief of police.

"Can I quote you on that, Sam?" he asked.

"No, you know darned well you can't!" Chief Reynolds exploded. "That's off the record. You boys! I forgot you were here! Don't go repeating what I've said, you hear?"

"We won't, sir," Jupiter assured him.

"Altogether," Chief Reynolds continued, "that green figure was seen by—let me see now. Two truckers at the diner. The woman who telephoned in. The night watchman at the warehouse. Myself and two of my men. The two boys——"

"That makes nine, Sam," Mr. Andrews put in.

"Nine, plus the six men who wandered over to look at the old place," Chief Reynolds said. "Fifteen altogether. Fifteen witnesses to a ghostly figure!"

"Were there six men at the Green mansion, Chief," Jupiter asked eagerly, "or seven? Pete and Bob can't agree."

"I'm not sure," the Chief grumbled. "Four men reported what happened. Three of them said there were six, and one said there were seven. I didn't talk to the others— couldn't locate them. Guess they didn't want publicity. But either way, there were fifteen or sixteen witnesses and that's too many to imagine something. I sure wish I could play it down as a gag or something, but after seeing it myself—watching it just disappear into a grave—well, I can't!"

Now the car turned up the weed-grown driveway of the old Green mansion. By daylight it looked very impressive, even though one wing was partly torn down. Two policemen stood guard at the door, and a man in a brown suit seemed to be waiting impatiently with them.

"Wonder who that is?" Chief Reynolds muttered as they got out. "Probably another reporter."

"Chief Reynolds!" The man in the brown suit, an intelligent looking man who spoke rapidly in a pleasant voice, came toward them. "Are you the chief? I've been waiting for you. Why won't these men let me go into my client's house?"

"Your client's house?" The chief stared at him. "Who're you?"

"I'm Harold Carlson," the man said. "Actually it is Miss Lydia Green's house. I'm her lawyer and also a distant cousin of hers. I represent her interests. As soon as I read this morning's paper about the events of last night, I flew straight down here from San Francisco, rented a car and drove out here. I want to investigate. The whole thing sounds like fantastic nonsense to me."

"Fantastic, yes," Chief Reynolds said, "but I don't think it's nonsense. Well, I'm mighty glad you're here, Mr. Carlson. We'd probably have had to send for you otherwise. I posted my men to keep out curiosity seekers and that's why they wouldn't let you in. But we'll all go in now and look around. I have here two boys who saw everything last night, and they'll point out exactly where the—er, strange manifestations took place."

He introduced Mr. Andrews, and Bob, Pete and Jupiter. Then Chief Reynolds led the way into the house, leaving his two men outside, on guard. Inside, in the big, dimly lit rooms, there was still a sense of the spookiness of the night before. Bob and Pete pointed out to the chief exactly where they had all been, and where the greenish figure had first appeared.

Then Pete led them upstairs.

"It just glided up these stairs and along the hall," he said. "Before we followed it, the men examined the floor for footprints. That was Bob's idea. But there wasn't a mark in the dust."

"Good work, son," Mr. Andrews said, and clapped Bob on the shoulder.

"Then the ghost went down that hall"—Pete pointed—"and stopped against the wall at the end. After that it just melted through the wall and vanished."

"Mmm." Chief Reynolds scowled as they all stood staring at the blank wall. Harold Carlson, the lawyer, was shaking his head helplessly.

"I don't understand it," he said. "I just don't understand it. Of course, there have always been stories about this house being haunted, but I never believed in them. Now—I don't know. I just don't know."

"Mr. Carlson," Chief Reynolds asked, "have you any idea what's behind that wall?"

The other man blinked. "Why—no. What could be behind it?"

"That's what we're here to find out," the chief said. "And why I'm glad you're here.

"This morning, one of the men engaged to wreck the house was working on a ladder, ripping some of the siding off the outside. Apparently this hallway is over the section downstairs that has been partly taken down, and this upper portion came next. Anyway, he saw something. And he stopped work and called me."

"Saw something?" Mr. Carlson frowned. "Good heavens, what?"

"He couldn't be sure," Chief Reynolds said bluntly.

"But he thinks there's a secret room behind that blank wall. And now that you're here, we're going to open it up and see what's inside."

Harold Carlson rubbed his forehead and looked at Mr. Andrews, who was busy making notes.

"A secret room?" he said, in utter bewilderment. "There's no mention of a secret room in any of the family stories about this house."

Pete and Bob and Jupiter were almost hopping with suppressed excitement as the two policemen came up the stairs, one carrying an axe and the other a crowbar.

"All right, men, get an opening in that wall," Chief Reynolds said. To Mr. Carlson he added, "I'm sure that's what you want, isn't it?"

"Of course, Chief," the man from San Francisco told him. "After all, the house is coming down anyway."

The two policemen attacked the wall with vigor. Soon they had a hole in it. It was plain that beyond it lay a sizeable space, now quite dark. When the hole was big enough for a man to get through, Chief Reynolds approached it and flashed a beam of light inside.

"Good grief!" he said and climbed through the opening into the secret room. Hastily Mr. Carlson and Bob's father followed him, and the boys could hear their exclamations of excitement and consternation from within.

Quietly Jupiter slipped through the hole, too, and after him Pete and Bob. They were in a small room, about six by eight. A little daylight came through a crack in the outside wall that the wreckers must have pulled loose.

It was no wonder the men were excited.

There was nothing in the room but a coffin.

It rested on two trestles, objects of polished wood similar to sawhorses. The coffin was magnificently carved and polished on the outside, but it was the inside that was now getting the men's attention.

The three boys crept up beside them and peered in also. All three gasped.

There was a skeleton in the coffin. They could not see it very well because of the magnificent robes, partly destroyed by age and decay, which hid it. But it was sure enough a skeleton.

For a moment no one said anything. Then Harold Carlson spoke.

"Look!" he said. "This silver plate on the coffin. It says, 'Beloved wife of Mathias Greene. Rest close by and undisturbed.'"

· "Old Mathias Green's Chinese wife!" Chief Reynolds said huskily.

"And everyone always thought she had run away when he died," Bob's father added, in a hushed tone.

"Yes," agreed Harold Carlson. "But look at this! This is something I'm going to have to take charge of, Chief, for the family."

He reached into the coffin. What he did the boys couldn't see because the bodies of the men blocked their view. But a moment later Mr. Carlson held up a long string

of round objects which were a curious dull gray color in the beam from the chief's flashlight.

"These must be the famous Ghost Pearls that Great-uncle Mathias is reported to have stolen from a Chinese noble. They were the reason he had to flee China and go into hiding. They're immensely valuable. We thought they were gone forever—that when Great-uncle Mathias broke his neck, his Chinese wife cleared out with the pearls and went back to the Orient.

"Instead, they've been here ever since."

"And so has she," Bob's father commented.

CHAPTER 4

An Unexpected Phone Call

In Headquarters, the next day, Pete was busy clipping stories and pictures from the newspapers while Bob pasted them in a large scrapbook. Mr. Andrews hadn't been able to do much about cutting down on the publicity Rocky Beach received in connection with the story of the Green mansion and the green ghost.

Probably the story of the ghost would not have held the public's interest very long. But when it was followed by the discovery of a secret room and the skeleton of Mathias Green's wife wearing a rope of famous pearls around her neck—some of the headlines seemed bigger than the front pages they were on.

Now the reporters were digging back into the past and recounting the events of Mathias Green's history. Their articles told that he had been a reckless captain in the China trade, and had sailed into the teeth of any storm he met, daring the elements to faze him.

They revealed that he had been a personal friend and adviser of several Manchu nobles, and that he had received gifts of jewels from them. But the Ghost Pearls hadn't been given to him. He had stolen them and then hastily left China with his bride, never to return. The rest of his life had been spent in seclusion in the Green mansion.

"Imagine all this happening right here in Rocky Beach!" Bob paused to exclaim. "You know what Dad and Chief Reynolds have figured out?"

He was interrupted by the scrape of metal. That was the iron grating over the outside entrance to Tunnel Two being moved aside. Then, presently, there was a muffled scrambling noise—that was Jupe crawling through the long corrugated pipe that formed Tunnel Two. And then came the code rap on the trap door, which now opened upward, to allow Jupiter to crawl in, looking sweaty and hot.

"Whew!" he said. "It's hot." Then he added, "I've been thinking."

"Better be careful, Jupe," Pete said. "Don't overdo it. By the sweat you're in, your brain bearings must have been overloaded. We wouldn't want them to burn out and leave you just an ordinary guy like the rest of us."

Bob chuckled. Pete was actually very proud of his

friend's mental ability. But Pete couldn't help cutting Jupe down to size once in a while. It didn't hurt any because Jupiter Jones was not by nature an especially modest boy.

Jupe gave Pete a sour look.

"I have been deducing." He lowered himself into the swivel chair behind the burned desk with which their Headquarters office was furnished. "I have been figuring out what happened there in the Green mansion many years ago."

"You don't have to, Jupe," Bob said. "My dad told me what he and Chief Reynolds have figured out."

"What I have decided," Jupe said, seeming not to hear Bob, "is that first——"

"Dad and Chief Reynolds agree that Mrs. Green probably died of some illness," Bob went right on. He was seldom in possession of inside information like this, and he didn't intend to be cheated out of telling it.

"Then her husband, the old sea captain, put her in that wonderful coffin but he couldn't bear to be really parted from her. So he put her in that little room at the end of the corridor and closed up the window. Then he plastered and papered over the door so no outsider would guess there was a secret room.

"That way she stayed with him, you might say. How long this lasted there's no way of guessing, but then one night Mathias Green stumbled coming down the stairs.

"When the servants saw he was dead, they panicked. They slipped away in the night. They either went up to

Chinatown in San Francisco and lost themselves there with their relatives, or they went back to China. Some of them may have been in this country illegally. In any case, Chinese in those days were very clannish and didn't give any information to white men if they could help it, so their running away was perfectly natural.

"The only relative was Mr. Green's sister-in-law, who inherited everything. She used the money to buy a big vineyard up near San Francisco—Verdant Valley Vineyard. She never came down here at all. Neither did Miss Lydia Green, her daughter, who owns Verdent Valley now and is the owner of the Green mansion since her mother died.

"For some unknown reason they just let the old house sit there all this time. Until this year Miss Green finally agreed to sell it to developers."

"And when they started to tear it down, old Mathias Green's ghost got annoyed," Pete put in. "That's why he screamed, and was seen going into the hidden room. He was paying a last visit to his wife. After that he—well, apparently he just left."

Jupiter looked slightly annoyed. This was just about what he had figured out himself. However, he contented himself by assuming an air of superiority.

"You seem pretty sure it was a ghost," he remarked. "And also that it was Mathias Green's ghost."

"We saw it. You didn't," Pete retorted. "If that wasn't a ghost, I've never seen one!"

Of course, he never had seen one—at least not previously. But he ignored that fact.

"If it wasn't a ghost, what was it?" Bob asked. "If you can think of any other possibility, Chief Reynolds would probably give you a reward."

Jupiter blinked. "What do you mean?"

"Yes," chimed in Pete, also looking interested. "What about the chief?"

"Well, we all heard him say yesterday he saw the ghost," Bob told them. "And Dad tells me the chief is pretty upset because officially he can't admit there is any such thing as a ghost. And so he can't order his men to try to catch it for him. But he still can't forget he saw it, and so maybe there *are* ghosts. He would certainly be grateful to anybody who could either prove it was a real ghost, or if it wasn't, exactly what it was we all saw."

"Mmm." Jupiter was beginning to look pleased. "I believe we should take on this case of the green ghost just as a favor to Police Chief Reynolds. Besides, I have a feeling there is a lot more to this mystery than any of us guess."

"Now wait a minute!" Pete yelled. "He hasn't asked us to take on any case for him. And I draw the line at investigating green ghosts!"

Bob, however, was as interested as Jupiter.

"Our motto is, 'We Investigate Anything,' " he reminded Pete. "I'd like to know for myself if we really saw a ghost or not. But how would we start trying to catch one?"

37

"We will review the case from the beginning," Jupiter said. "First, was the ghost seen again last night?"

"Not according to the papers," Bob said. "And Dad said he heard from Chief Reynolds that no new reports have come in."

"Did your father interview the men who saw the phantom figure the other night?" Jupiter asked Bob.

"He went around with Chief Reynolds," Bob answered. "They could only find four of them. The big man, the man with the little dog, and two neighbors. They all said the same thing—exactly what I've put in my notes."

"What about the other two?—— Or three?"

"They couldn't locate them. Dad said they probably didn't want publicity, didn't want to be kidded by their friends about seeing a ghost. Though I'm sure there were three others, not two."

"How did these men come to visit the old Green mansion anyway?" Jupe asked.

"They all said a couple of men came along from up the road and suggested they all go see the mansion by moonlight before it was torn down. They made it seem like a good idea. So the men went. As they came up the driveway, they heard the scream, and you know the rest."

"Has the wrecking of the mansion stopped?" Jupiter asked.

"For the time being, anyway," Bob said. "The chief has had the house searched for more secret rooms, but there aren't any. Still, he's having it guarded against sightseers and Dad said there was some talk that the whole deal for tearing it down and building a new development might fall through now, because of the bad publicity."

Jupiter thought hard for several minutes.

"Well," he said finally, "we might as well play over the tape you recorded, Bob. It's just about all we have in the way of clues."

Bob switched on the tape recorder. Once again the eerie scream rang in their ears. Then they heard the conversation of the men who had joined them that night. Listening, Jupiter frowned.

"Something about that tape stirs an adea in my mind," he said, "but I can't quite get it. I heard a dog bark a little. What kind of dog was it?"

"What difference does it make what kind of dog it was?" Pete exploded.

"Anything may be important, Pete," Jupiter said loftily.

"It was a little wire-haired fox terrier," Bob told him. "Do you have any ideas yet, Jupe?"

Jupiter was forced to admit he didn't. They played the tape again, and again. Something about it bothered Jupe, but he couldn't figure what it was. Finally they put the recorder away and began to study the newspaper clippings, one by one.

"It certainly looks to me as if the green ghost had moved out of town," Pete said finally, with satisfaction. "They were tearing his house down so he left!"

Jupe was trying to think of an answer to that when the

phone rang. He picked it up.

"Hello?" he said. They could all hear the conversation through the loudspeaker attachment he had rigged up on the telephone.

"This is long distance," a woman's voice said. "I have a call for Robert Andrews."

The boys stared at each other. It was the first long distance call any of them had ever had.

"For you, Bob," Jupiter handed Bob the receiver.

"Hello," Bob said. "This is Bob Andrews." His voice squeaked slightly from excitement.

"Hello, Bob." It was another woman's voice that spoke. This one was obviously quite an old woman, though her voice was strong. "This is Miss Lydia Green, calling from Verdant Valley."

Lydia Green! The niece of old Mathias Green whose ghost—if it was a ghost—Bob and Pete had seen!

"Yes, Miss Green," he said.

"I want to ask a favor of you," Miss Green said over the phone. "Could you and your friend, Peter Crenshaw, come to Verdant Valley?"

"Come to Verdant Valley?" Bob asked in bewilderment.

"I very much want to talk to you," Miss Green said. "You saw my uncle's—well, his ghost two nights ago and I want all the details from an eye witness. What he looked like, what he did, everything. You see——" and for a moment her voice faltered—"you see, the ghost has come to Verdant Valley. Last night I—I saw him in my room."

CHAPTER 5

The Ghost Appears Again

Bob looked at Jupiter. Jupe was nodding his head, to say yes.

"Why, sure, Miss Green," Bob said into the phone. "I guess Pete and I could come. That is if it's all right with our families."

"Oh, I'm so glad!" Miss Green seemed to sigh with relief. "Naturally I called your families first and your mothers said they were sure it would be all right. Verdant Valley is a very peaceful place, and I have a great-nephew here, Charles Chang Green, who will be company for you. He has spent most of his life in China."

The rest of Miss Green's call was about arrangements. Bob and Pete were to catch the 6 P.M. jet flight to San Francisco, and she would have them met at the airport

41

and driven to Verdant Valley. Then she thanked them again, and hung up.

"Gleeps!" Bob said. "She wants to know all about the ghost from an eye witness so we get a nice trip out of it!" The realization struck him. "But she didn't invite you, Jupe!"

If Jupe was disappointed, he was working hard to conceal it.

"That's because I didn't see the ghost," he said. "You two did. Anyway, I couldn't go because tomorrow Uncle Titus and Aunt Mathilda are driving down to San Diego in the big truck to buy a lot of Navy surplus material, and I have to stay to take care of the business."

"Just the same, we're a team," Pete objected. "I hate to be going someplace without you, Jupe. Especially," he added, "if there's going to be a ghost around!"

Jupiter pinched his lip.

"Perhaps this is a fortunate circumstance," he said. "If the ghost has been seen up in Verdant Valley, you two can carry out an investigation there for Chief Reynolds. Meanwhile, I'll follow up all the leads I can think of here. The value of having a team of investigators is that we can follow up two or even three different lines of investigation at the same time."

They left it at that. After all, what Jupe said made sense. Presently Bob and Pete rode home to get ready. Their mothers had packed suitcases for them, and the boys made sure to add a flashlight, and to be certain each of them carried his special piece of chalk—green for Bob, blue for Pete—for leaving the sign of The Three Investigators, when necessary.

Mrs. Andrews drove them to Los Angeles' busy, modern International Airport, and Jupiter came along.

"Phone me any developments," he told Bob. "We have some money saved up to pay for calls. If the ghost is really up there, I'll think of some way to get there to join you."

Mrs. Andrews' final words to Bob were, "Now be sure to watch your manners, Robert. And if you can tell Miss Green anything that will help her, I'll be very glad, though I have to admit this whole business is very puzzling. Even your father says he thinks there is a lot more to it than meets the eye.

"But Miss Green has a fine reputation, and her Verdant Valley Vineyard is known to be well-run. It's a winery, too, because they make wine out of the grapes. I think they call it the Three-V Winery. They have horses, Miss Green said, so you two and the great-nephew she mentioned can go riding together. You should have a nice time."

A few moments later they were on the plane, and the great jet was in the air, arrowing northward. The trip only took an hour, which hardly gave them time to get used to it, especially since part of it was taken up by a dinner, served on plastic trays.

Then they went back to watching the ground flow by

underneath them until they swooped in for a landing at the San Francisco airport.

They were met by a boy almost as tall as Pete, but with broader shoulders, who stepped forward to greet them. He was a good-looking youth, who seemed very American except for the slight Oriental appearance of his eyes.

He introduced himself as Charles Green, better known as Chang, told them he was one-quarter Chinese and had lived most of his life in Hong Kong. Then he helped them get their bags from the luggage section. When they had their suitcases, Chang Green led them across a busy street to a huge parking lot.

Here a small, bus-type station wagon was waiting, with a young man who looked Mexican at the wheel.

"Pedro, these are our guests, Pete Crenshaw and Bob Andrews. We'll go straight back to Verdant Valley. They ate on the plane so we don't have to stop."

"Si, Señor Chang," Pedro said. He grabbed the boy's bags, stowed them in the back and took his place behind the wheel. The three boys took their places directly behind him, where they could sit side by side, Pedro threw in the gears and they were off.

During the ride, Pete and Bob tried to talk and ask questions and look around them, all at the same time. Somewhat to their disappointment, they did not go into the city of San Francisco itself, but skirted its edges and then were rolling through hilly but more or less open country.

44

"We are going to Verdant Valley, where my honorable aunt operates the 3-V Winery," Chang Green said. "Actually, my aunt says that I am the rightful owner of the vineyard and winery, but I could not dream of taking them away from her."

At this statement, Pete and Bob looked at him with new interest. They waited for him to explain, and he did, as they sped along.

It turned out that Chang was actually the great-grandson of old Mathias Green. Mathias Green had taken as his second wife the Chinese princess whose skeleton the boys had helped find. His first wife had traveled with him on all his voyages, and she had died of a fever during one voyage to the Orient, leaving him with a small son, Elija, to bring up.

Unable to care for the boy, Mathias had placed him in an American mission school in Hong Kong to be reared and educated. Then, a short time later, Mathias had gotten himself into trouble with the authorities for illegally taking the Ghost Pearl necklace, had married a beautiful young Chinese princess, and had hurriedly sailed back for America, leaving his son still in Hong Kong.

Elija Green, whose father never sent for him, had grown up to become an American medical missionary in China and had married a Chinese wife. When they both died of yellow fever, their son Thomas in turn had been brought up in the American mission school. Thomas, Chang's father, had known nothing of his American relatives, for

45

his father had refused ever to speak of Mathias Green. He, too, had spent his entire life in China as a doctor. He had married an English missionary's daughter, and they had been very happy until a flood in the Yellow River had overturned their boat, and they had drowned.

Chang paused as he said this, and Pete and Bob could see him swallow hard.

"Those were troubled times in China," he said. "I was just a baby and I was rescued from the flood by a Chinese family with whom I had lived for several years. Then they heard that my life was in danger because I was an American, and they slipped into Hong Kong with me, to safety.

"I did not know my real name then, so for some years I grew up in a missionary school, just as my father and grandfather had done. Then one of my teachers, when I told him my mother's and father's first names, which I remembered, looked up the old records and told me that my real name was Green. He got in touch with Aunt Lydia in this country, and she sent for me.

"I have been living with her ever since. She has been very kind to me and I want very much to help her, because she is so upset now. Uncle Harold also is trying to help her, but he is deeply troubled, too. Now come these stories of my great-grandfather's ghost appearing, and everything is much worse. I cannot explain it all now, for there is much I do not understand, but you will see for yourselves."

Bob started to ask a question. But he couldn't remem-

46

ber what it was. It had been an exciting day, and an exciting trip, and now the swift motion of the little auto bus was a soothing one. His eyes closed, and he fell asleep.

He woke with a start when they stopped. The sun had set behind a high ridge. They were in front of a large, old house, built of stone and timber, on a little spot behind which the mountain ridge rose abruptly. Apparently they were in a long, narrow valley. He could not see too much because the valley was already in deep twilight, but he could make out what looked like miles of cultivated ground where small bushes grew, undoubtedly grape vines.

"Wake up!" Pete said. "We're here."

Bob stifled a yawn as he came fully awake. He clambered out. Chang led them up a long flight of wooden steps to the porch of the old house.

"This is Verdant House," Chang told him. "Verdant, as I'm sure you know, means green. My aunt chose that name for the vineyard and the house because our name is Green. Now you will meet her. I know she is anxious to see you."

They entered a big hall paneled in redwood, and a tall, dignified, rather frail-looking woman came out of a room to great them.

"Good evening, boys," she said. "I'm so glad you are here. Did you have a good trip?"

They assured her they had, and she led them into a dining room.

"I know you're probably hungry," she said. "Even

47

though you may have eaten earlier. Boys are always hungry. So I'm going to leave you to eat something and get acquainted with Chang. We'll talk tomorrow. Today has been a very busy and troublesome day and I am rather tired. I'm going to bed early."

She beat on a small bronze Chinese gong, and an elderly Chinese woman came into the room.

"You may serve supper now, Li," Miss Green said. "Chang will probably be ready to eat another meal, too."

"All' boys all time starve," said the shriveled little Chinese woman. "I feed um good."

She bustled out. As she did so, a man entered the room. Bob and Pete recognized him as Harold Carlson, whom they had seen in Rocky Beach the day before, when the skeleton in the secret room had been discovered. He looked worried.

"Hello, boys," he said in his light, pleasant voice. "Never dreamed when we met yesterday under such strange circumstances we'd be meeting again here. But——" He paused and shook his head. "Frankly," he sighed, "*I* don't know what to make of it. Neither does anyone else."

"Good night, boys," Miss Green said. "I'm going up to bed. Harold, will you assist me?"

"Certainly, Aunt Lydia." The man took Miss Green's elbow lightly and walked with her out of the room and up the stairs. Chang switched on the lights.

"It gets dark suddenly here in the valley," he said.

"It's practically night outside now. Well, let us eat and I'll try to tell you some more about us. Perhaps you'd like to ask questions?"

"No time talk, talk, talk!" exclaimed the Chinese woman, Li, as she pushed a serving cart into the room. "Now time for boys to eat. Eat to make big men. Come sit down."

She put a platter of cold roast beef, plates of bread and pickles and potato salad and other cold dishes on the table. Bob suddenly realized that he was starved. That meal on the plane seemed a long time ago, and awfully small, too.

He and the others started toward the table.

But their meal was to be postponed.

Just as they started to sit down, they heard a piercing scream from upstairs. It was followed by an ominous silence.

"That was Aunt Lydia!" Chang cried, jumping up. "Something's wrong!"

He ran for the stairs. Bob and Pete automatically followed him, and so did Li and several other servants who appeared from nowhere.

Chang led the way up the stairs and down a hall. At the end of the hall a door was open, the light on, and they could see Harold Carlson bending over Miss Green, who lay stretched out on a bed. He was massaging her wrists and speaking to her urgently.

"Aunt Lydia!" he said. "Aunt Lydia, can you hear

me?" He saw the others "Li!" he said. "Bring missy's smelling salts!"

The old Chinese woman scurried into a bathroom and came back with a small bottle. While the others crowded at the door, she held the open bottle under Miss Green's nose. After a moment Miss Green shuddered slightly and opened her eyes.

"I've been foolish, haven't I?" she said. "I fainted? Yes, I screamed and fainted. It's the first time in my life I ever fainted."

"But what happened, Aunt Lydia?" Chang asked anxiously. "Why did you scream?"

"I saw the ghost again," Miss Green said, trying to keep her voice steady. "After I said good night to Harold, and entered my room, just before I turned on the light, I looked toward that alcove."

She pointed to a small alcove near the windows.

"And the ghost was standing there, as clear as day. It looked at me with terrible, burning eyes. It wore green robes, just as Uncle Mathias used to, and I'm sure it was he, although the face was just a misty blur, except for the burning eyes."

Her voice dropped to a whisper. "He is angry at me. I know he is. You see, many years ago my mother promised him that after his death the mansion in Rocky Beach would be closed and never opened again. She made a solemn vow that neither the house nor the ground it was built on would be sold or disturbed in any way. And I have broken that promise. I agreed to sell the house, and now the body of Uncle Mathias' bride has been disturbed and he—he is angry at me!"

CHAPTER 6

Startling Developments

Supper, when Pete and Bob and Chang finally got to it, was gobbled in bites between bursts of excited talk.

Miss Green had been put to bed with a soothing drink by Li, who seemed to be a combined cook and house-keeper. When the servants had been sent about their business with stern orders to say nothing of what had happened—orders bound to be disobeyed—the boys went back to the dining room.

Mr. Carlson joined them, looking very upset.

"Did you see the ghost, sir?" Pete asked.

Harold Carlson shook his head.

"I just saw Aunt Lydia to her room," he said. "It was dark and she went in alone. I was just turning away when she screamed. Her door was partly open and as I turned,

I saw the light go on. Apparently she had had her finger on the light switch, and when she saw the—well, whatever she saw, she unconsciously finished turning on the light. Naturally with the bright light on, there was nothing to see or at least I couldn't see anything.

"She had her hand to her mouth, horrified. Then, as I rushed in, she slumped in a faint and I was there just in time to catch her. I put her on her bed and was rubbing her wrists to revive her when you arrived.

He rubbed his forehead with a worried hand.

"The servants are bound to talk," he said. "It's impossible to shut them up. By morning the story that the ghost has been seen will be all over Verdant Valley."

"Are you worried because maybe the newspapers will learn about it and print the story?" Bob asked.

"The newspapers have already done as much harm as they can do," the man replied. "I'm worried about the effect on our workers. I believe Aunt Lydia told you over the phone that she saw the ghost in her room last night also?"

Bob and Pete nodded.

"Well, two of the maids saw it, too, or they say they saw it—outside, on the patio, where they were sitting and chattering. They were frightened half out of their wits. I thought I had persuaded them that they had imagined it, but I guess I didn't because this morning there were rumors all over the valley about the ghost having moved here from Rocky Beach. All our workers were buzzing with gossip about it.

"You think that the ghost will frighten the workers, is that it, Uncle Harold?" Chang asked.

"Yes!" the man burst out. "That ghost will ruin us! Ruin us completely!"

Then, as if he regretted the outburst, his voice became calmer.

"But that's not the concern of our guests. Perhaps you boys would like to see the pearls that I recovered yesterday when you were present?

Bob and Pete agreed they would. They had only had a glimpse of them there in the secret room in the Green mansion.

Mr. Carlson led the way out of the dining room and down a hall into a small office, equipped with a big roll-top desk, a number of filing cabinets, a telephone, and a large, old-fashioned safe in the corner.

He knelt and spun the dial of the safe. In a moment, he rejoined them carrying a small cardboard box, which he placed on the desk and opened. Then he lifted out the necklace inside and placed it on the green blotter of the desk, where it showed up clearly.

Bob and Pete leaned over, and Chang joined them. The pearls were large, but all of them were irregular in shape and had a strange, dull gray color. They were not at all like the lustrous, round pink-white pearls in the small string Bob's mother owned.

"That's a funny color for pearls," Pete said.

"It's why they are called Ghost Pearls," Mr. Carlson told them. "I believe all such pearls came from one tiny bay in the Indian Ocean, and are no longer found. In the Orient rich nobles value them highly, but I don't know why because their shape is not perfect and their color is very unattractive. Just the same, their value is high. I'm sure these could be sold for a hundred thousand dollars or more."

"In that case, Uncle Harold," Chang began, "Aunt Lydia could pay off the debts she owes and save the vineyard and the winery!" And he added, "Surely the pearls now belong to her!"

"There's a complication." Mr. Carlson shook his head. "Obviously Mathias Green gave these pearls to his Chinese wife. So they were hers, not his. By the laws of inheritance, if you can follow me, they would belong to *her* nearest relative."

"But her family disowned her," Chang said, puzzled. "They said she was no longer a daughter. Besides, since the revolution and war in China, her family has vanished."

"I know." Mr. Carlson mopped his brow. "Just the same, I have had a letter from a Chinese lawyer in San Francisco who claims he has a client who is a descendant of the bride's sister. He warns me to keep the pearls safe because his client claims them. The whole matter will have to be tried in court and it may take years before we know to whom the pearls belong."

Chang's brow furrowed. He seemed about to say some-

56

thing when outside in the hall they heard hurrying footsteps. A strong knock sounded on the door.

"Come in!" Harold Carlson said, as they all turned.

The door opened and a burly, middle-aged man with swarthy features and piercing eyes came in. He was breathless as he spoke, ignoring the boys.

"Mr. Carlson, sir, the ghost has been seen down by the Number One pressing house. Three Mexican grape pickers saw it, and they have panicked. You'd better come."

"Oh, this is terrible! I'll be right with you, Jensen," Mr. Carlson groaned. Hurriedly he put the necklace back in the safe and swung the door shut. Then, with the three boys at their heels, he and the other man hurried out of the house to a waiting jeep. They all managed to climb in, Bob sitting on Pete's lap, and the little vehicle took off with a roar, spinning around and dashing through the darkness down the alley.

Bob and Pete were too busy holding on as the jeep bumped along the dirt road to have seen much even if it hadn't been night. But the ride only lasted five minutes. Then they came to a skidding stop outside a low building that the headlights showed to be made of concrete and concrete bricks. It looked new.

They all got out. The smell of grapes, and of freshly pressed grape juice, was heavy in the air.

"Mr. Jensen is the foreman of the planting and picking operation," Chang whispered to the boys as they got out. "He oversees the labor force for that part of the operation."

Mr. Jensen shut off the headlights, just as a young man, somewhat raggedly dressed, came forward from the darkness around the building.

"Well, Henry?" Mr. Jensen barked at him. "See anything since I left?"

The young man shook his head.

"No, sir, Mr. Jensen," he said. "Not anything, sir."

"Where are those three pickers?" Jensen asked. The young man was now close enough for them to see him spread his hands.

"Who knows?" he said. "They fled as soon as you left. They ran, and"—he chuckled—"I have never seen them run before. Probably they are in Verdant," he pointed toward the little cluster of lights at the other end of the valley, "in a café telling everyone that they saw the ghost."

"That's just what I didn't want," Mr. Jensen said grimly. "You should have stopped them."

"I tried to speak sense to them," the young man said. "They would not listen. Fear had turned their minds."

"The fat's in the fire all right," Harold Carlson said dejectedly. "What were those men doing down here after dark anyway?"

"I told them to meet me here, sir," Jensen reported. "They are the ones who have been mainly responsible for spreading stories about the ghost, and I wanted a chance to tell them to keep their mouths shut or be fired. But I was delayed getting here and while they waited for me, they imagined they saw something.

"I'm sure that's just what it was—imagination. They've been talking so much about ghosts that they thought they saw one."

"Whether it was imagination or not, the harm is done," Mr. Carlson said. "Maybe you can go into the village and calm them down, though that's probably hopeless."

"Yes, sir. Shall I drive you all back to the house first?"

"Yes, and——" Harold Carlson clapped his hand against his forehead with an exclamation. "Good heavens!" he cried. "Chang! Did I lock the safe after I put the pearls back?"

"I don't know, sir," Chang replied. "Your back hid the safe. I couldn't see."

"I could," Pete spoke up. He was trying hard to search his memory for what he had actually seen back in the office. "You put the pearls inside—and you slammed the door shut and turned the handle——"

"Yes, yes," Harold Carlson broke in. "But did I turn the dial?"

Pete thought hard. He couldn't be sure. And yet—

"No, Mr. Carlson," he said finally. "I don't think you did."

"I don't think I did either," Harold Carlson groaned. "I went away and left the safe unlocked with the Ghost Pearls in it. Jensen, quick, get me back to the house. Then you can come back and pick up the boys."

"Right. Here, Chang, take my flashlight." Jensen

pressed a powerful flashlight into Chang Green's hand, then the two men leaped into the jeep and roared off.

"Golly!" Bob broke the silence that followed. "First up at the house. Now down here. But why is everybody so worried about people talking, Chang?"

Unconsciously the three boys had drawn close together in the silent darkness, broken only by the sound of insects.

"It is because the grape-picking season has commenced," Chang said. "Now the grapes are ripening and must be picked and brought to the presses to have the juice extracted. Every day more grapes ripen, and if they are not picked, soon they are too ripe for good wine, or else they rot.

"It takes many men to pick the grapes, but it is not a year-round job, so we have many workers who come here just for the picking season, then go elsewhere. Some are Mexicans, some are Americans, some are of Oriental ancestry, but they are all poor, hard-working people who are very superstitious.

"The pickers have been uneasy since the stories first appeared in the papers of the green ghost in Rocky Beach. Now, if the ghost is here in Verdant Valley, many of the pickers will flee in superstitious fear. They will quit their jobs, and we will not be able to get other pickers. The grapes will rot on the vines, we will not be able to press the juice, and the crop will be a failure. The 3-V Winery will lose much money—and I am sure my aunt is worried because a great deal of money is owed and every penny counts."

"Gosh, that's tough," Pete said in awkward sympathy. "All because they started to tear down your great-grandfather's house and his ghost started roaming."

"No!" Chang said stubbornly. "I do not believe it is my great-grandfather's honorable spirit. He would not wish to do harm to those of his own family. It is some other evil spirit seeking to work mischief."

He spoke with such conviction that Bob wanted to believe him. But he had been at the Green mansion and he had seen that misty figure in the flowing Mandarin robes, and he was afraid Chang was wrong.

The three boys were silent a moment longer, trying to decide what to do next. It was Bob who spoke first.

"If the ghost was seen here," he said, "then we ought to look around and see if we can see it again."

"Well——" Pete's voice sounded reluctant— "I guess that makes sense. But I sure wish Jupe were here."

"The ghost has harmed no one," Chang said. "It has only shown itself. We need not fear it. And if it is the honorable spirit of my ancestor, it cannot intend harm. I agree, Bob. Let us look around the pressing house and see if the ghost still lingers there."

He led the boys in a slow circle around the building. He seemed to know his way well, and did not turn on the flashlight because, as he said, light would make it impossible to see the green ghost.

They strained their eyes, watching, but saw nothing

except the darker shadow of the building in the dark night. Chang explained as they walked, telling them it was a new pressing house. "Here is where the ripe grapes are put into big tanks. Large rotary paddles crush the grapes and press out the juice, which flows to a gathering tank. From the gathering tank it is pumped into vats in the aging cellars. These are really caves cut into the nearby mountain, where the temperature and humidity remained constant all year round."

Bob was only half listening. He was straining to catch a glimpse of anything that might look like a glowing figure, but they circled the building completely without seeing anything.

"Perhaps we should go inside," Chang finally suggested. "I will show you the machinery and the tanks. It is all very new. It was just built last year when Uncle Harold bought much new machinery, and a great deal of money is owed. That is why my honorable aunt worries so. She is afraid she cannot repay the money."

But at that moment headlights came into sight and a moment later the jeep pulled up beside them.

"Hop in, boys," Jensen said. "I'll take you back to the house. First, though, I have to do an errand in the village. I have to try to find those three pickers who claim they saw the ghost, make them keep their mouths shut, and try to undo the damage they've already done."

"Thank you, Mr. Jensen," Chang said. "We can walk. It's only a little over a mile. Here's your flashlight. The moon is up now so we can see the road easily."

"Anything you say," the burly man agreed. "I only hope those three haven't panicked all our pickers, or there won't be a dozen showing up tomorrow."

The jeep roared off down the valley toward a small cluster of lights which must have been the village the man had referred to. Pete turned to Bob.

"You don't mind walking, do you, Bob?" he asked.

"My leg feels fine," Bob told him. He explained to Chang, "When I was a little kid I rolled down a hill and broke my leg in about umpteen pieces. I had to wear a brace until just last week. But Dr. Alvarez took it off and said I was okay now, that exercise would do my leg good."

"We will not hurry," Chang said, and they started strolling down the dusty road in the moonlight, smelling the ripe grapes all around them. Chang was silent for some moments.

"Excuse me," he said at last. "I have just been thinking of the way in which this ghost business will be a disaster for the Verdant Valley. All our pickers will desert, as I said. The crop will rot. We will lose a great deal of money. Aunt Lydia will not be able to pay off the notes she signed, and Verdant Valley will be taken away from her.

"That is why I was silent. I was worrying for her sake. I know how much the vineyard and the winery mean to her. After all, first her mother, and then Aunt Lydia, spent their lives in building up the business. To lose it now will crush her. There is one hope. If we can clear up the title to the Ghost Pearls, and prove they do not belong to someone else, she can sell them for a great deal of money and pay off the debts."

"I sure hope you can," Pete said. "But what do you really think, Chang? Is it your great-grandfather's ghost we've been seeing, or what?"

"I do not know," the other boy answered slowly. "I cannot believe my grandfather's spirit would mean harm, even though he was a rough man in life. In China I learned not to disbelieve in spirits, either good ones or evil ones. I think this is an evil spirit at work, and not my great-grandfather at all. Yes, it is an evil spirit!"

By now they had reached the house. A few lights were on, but everything seemed very quiet. They climbed the stairs, entered, and went in. Chang seemed surprised to find the big living room empty.

"The servants have all gone to bed," he said, "but I was sure Uncle Harold would be here. He said he wanted to ask you some questions. Perhaps he is in his office."

He led them down the hall to the office. The door was shut. Chang knocked. The only answer they got was a muffled groan and a bumping noise.

Alarmed, Chang thrust the door open. All three boys stared at the sight of Harold Carlson lying on the floor, his wrists and ankles tightly tied and brought together behind his back. A brown paper bag covered his head.

"Uncle Harold!" Chang cried.

He rushed in, Bob and Pete at his heels, and snatched

64

off the paper bag. Harold Carlson's eyes bulged up at them, and he tried to utter words through a thick gag that filled his mouth.

"Don't try to talk, we'll cut you free!" Chang said swiftly.

He whipped out a pocket knife and cut loose the gag, made of a bandanna. Then, as Harold Carlson gasped for breath, he freed the man's legs and wrists. Mr. Carlson sat up, rubbing his wrists.

"What happened?" Pete asked.

"When I returned to the house and entered the office, someone was hiding behind the door. Whoever it was grabbed me from behind, held me while a second man gagged me and tied me. Then they threw me on the floor and tied my ankles and wrists together and put a paper bag over my head. I heard the safe clang open—the safe!"

In sudden anxiety he turned and rushed to the big iron safe. They could all see it was open an inch or two. Mr. Carlson jerked the door wide open and reached in. His hands came out empty.

He stared at them, his lips working, his face gray.

"The Ghost Pearls!" he said huskily. "They've been stolen!"

CHAPTER 7

Jupiter Makes Deductions

Back in Rocky Beach, sitting alone in the living room of the cottage where he lived with his Uncle Titus and Aunt Mathilda, Jupiter Jones had been pinching his lip and thinking hard for an hour. Now he abruptly straightened up and screamed as loudly as he could. Then, pink-faced from the effort, he sat back and waited.

A moment later there was the sound of footsteps outside. The front door burst open and Konrad, the big, blond yard helper, thrust his head in. Hans, his brother, was in San Diego with the Joneses. Konrad's eyes bulged as he gaped at Jupiter.

"Who was that yelling just now, Jupe?" he asked excitedly.

"That was me," Jupiter said. "So you heard me?"

"Sure bet I heard you!" Konrad said emphatically. "Your window open, my window open, I heard you okay. Sound like you sat on a big tack or stubbed your toe or something."

Jupiter looked at the window behind him. It was wide open. His round face registered vexation.

"What you yell for, Jupe?" Konrad asked. "I don't see anything wrong."

"There isn't anything wrong except I forgot the window was open," Jupiter told him.

"Then why you yell?" Konrad persisted.

"I was practicing screaming," Jupiter told him.

"You sure you hokay, Jupe?" Konrad asked. "Not sick or something?"

"I'm fine," Jupiter told him. You can go back to your cottage now, I won't scream anymore tonight."

"That's good," Konrad said. "You sure scared me."

He closed the door and returned to the small cottage he shared with his brother Hans, about fifty yards behind the Joneses' home.

Jupiter sat where he was, his brain buzzing. An idea was trying to break through in his mind—an idea about the green ghost, but it wouldn't come. Presently he sighed and gave up. It was time for bed anyway.

As he stood up to go upstairs, he wondered what Bob and Pete were doing up in Verdant Valley.

As if in answer to his thoughts, the telephone rang. It was a collect call from Bob. Jupe accepted the call eagerly.

"What's happened, Bob?" he asked. "Did you see the green ghost?"

"No, but Miss Green saw it," Bob said excitedly. "And then you'll never guess what happened. The——"

"You are excited," Jupiter told him. "Please tell me everything that happened, slowly and in sequence. Don't skip any details."

This was not easy for Bob to do, because he wanted to get right to the fact that the Ghost Pearls had been stolen. However, Jupiter had been training him to get all facts in order, and not to skip anything because small details could turn out to be very important. So now he began with their meeting with Chang Green, and told Jupiter everything he could remember, just as it had happened.

Finally, to his great relief, he got to the theft of the pearls, and told about that.

"Hmmm," Jupiter said, as Bob paused for breath. "That is an unexpected development. What's happening now? Is an investigation being made?"

"Mr. Carlson sent for the local sheriff, Sheriff Bixby," Bob told him. "Sheriff Bixby is pretty old and doesn't seem to know what to do. The house here isn't in any town, so there isn't any police force to call on. Just the sheriff and a deputy who keeps saying, 'I'll be danged.'

"The sheriff has a theory, though. He thinks that with all the publicity in the papers about the pearls, some criminals from the city came down here to steal them. When they saw Mr. Carlson rush out, they slipped in through a window from the side porch. They got the pearls and were searching for anything else that might be valuable when Mr. Carlson came back unexpectedly. They grabbed him as he came in, gagged him and put a paper bag over his head, so he couldn't see a thing. All Mr. Carlson can tell us is that one of them was rather short, but very powerful. The sheriff says they're probably halfway back to the city by now. He's going to phone to the police in San Francisco, but he doesn't think it will do much good."

Jupiter pinched his lip. The sheriff's theory certainly sounded reasonable. With all the publicity the Ghost Pearls had had, it would probably have been surprising if some city thieves hadn't taken the opportunity to try to steal them. It was just bad luck that Mr. Carlson, in his excitement, had left the safe unlocked to make things easier for them.

And yet Jupiter couldn't help wondering if there might not be some connection between the green ghost and the theft of the jewels. He couldn't imagine what it could be, but he wondered.

"You and Pete keep your eyes open, Bob," he said at last. "I certainly wish I was there," he added, wistfully, "but I have to stay here because Uncle Titus and Aunt Mathilda will be away for at least another day. Phone me if anything else happens."

With that he hung up. He was tempted to stay up and think about what Bob had told him, but sleepiness overcame him. He went up to bed and tumbled in, to sleep heav-

70

ily with many dreams, in one of which he kept hearing a voice he almost recognized but didn't.

The following morning, he could not remember what he had been dreaming about.

Jupiter hoped it would be a quiet day at The Jones Salvage Yard, so he could think about all Bob had told him the previous evening.

However, as things usually happen, it was a very busy day at the salvage yard. Jupiter had to run the whole place, with Konrad's help, and he didn't have a minute to be alone and think. But at about five o'clock business slacked off. Jupiter made a swift decision. An idea had come to him—an important idea.

"Konrad," he said to the big yard helper, "you take charge. Close up at six o'clock. I have some investigating to do."

"Hokay, Jupe," the man said good-naturedly. "I do my best."

Jupiter hopped on his bike and sped across town to the wooded area near a small stream which was the site of the Green mansion. As he rode up the driveway, he saw a police car parked in front of it. A uniformed policeman leaned out the window of the car as Jupiter rode up. It was one of the men who had been at the house the previous morning.

"Just keep right on riding, sonny," the policeman said, a bit wearily. "I've been shooing sightseers and souvenir hunters away all day."

71

Jupiter got off his bike and reached into his pocket.

"A lot of people have been out here?" he asked.

"Ever since the ghost was seen," the policeman said. "We've had to guard this place to keep souvenir hunters from tearing it down. Now run along, I'm tired of shooing people off."

"I'm not here for souvenirs," Jupiter said. "Didn't you see me come here yesterday with Chief Reynolds when the secret room was discovered?"

The officer took a better look at him.

"Well, yes, now you mention it," he said. "You did come with the chief."

Jupiter took out a card and handed it to the officer. It was one of the firm's business cards. It said:

THE THREE INVESTIGATORS
"We Investigate Anything"
? ? ?

First Investigator. . . . . Jupiter Jones
Second Investigator. . . . . Pete Crenshaw
Records and Research . . . . Bob Andrews

The officer started to grin, then stopped. After all, Jupiter had come in the chief's car the previous day.

"You investigate things, huh?" he asked. "You investigating something for the chief?"

"I'm making an investigation that I'm sure will interest him if my idea works out," Jupiter said.

He told the officer what he wanted to do, and the man

nodded.

"That sounds all right," he said. "Go ahead in."

Jupiter trudged up the flagstone path to the house, studying it. It was solidly built, and the wing that was partly torn down showed that the walls were thick.

He went inside. He did not waste time looking around for more secret rooms or anything like that, because Chief Reynolds had said a thorough search of the house had been made. Instead, he went upstairs to the upper hall. There he stood on the top step, faced downstairs—and screamed.

He waited a minute, then went downstairs and in the lower hall screamed again. After that he went outdoors and walked down to the waiting policeman.

"Well?" he asked. "Could you hear me?"

"I heard a couple of yells," the officer told him. "One very faint one and one a little louder. The door was shut."

"The door was shut the night the ghost appeared," Jupiter said. He looked around. There was a big clump of ornamental bushes at the corner of the house. "Listen this time," he requested, and headed for the clump.

He stationed himself behind it, then leaned out a bit and gave another loud yell. When he walked back to the police car, the officer nodded.

"I heard that all right," he said, "loud and clear. Say, what are you trying to prove, anyway?"

"I'm trying to deduce where the ghost was when it screamed," Jupiter said. "According to my observations it

73

must have been outside the house. If it was inside, it would have had to have a very powerful pair of lungs."

"I don't know whether ghosts have lungs or not," the policeman chuckled, but Jupiter didn't smile.

"That's exactly the point," he said, and the man scratched his head. Jupiter started toward his bike, but the officer called after him.

"Say," he called, "what are the question marks on your card for?"

Jupiter suppressed a chuckle. Those question marks always attracted attention.

"The question mark," he said, in a very adult manner, "is our symbol, our trademark. It stands for mysteries unsolved, enigmas unanswered, conundrums requiring an answer."

He got on his bike, leaving the officer still scratching his head, and rode away. He rode only a few blocks, however. By then he was away from the extensive grounds of the old Green mansion, and in a neatly built, modern suburb.

He had with him a clipping from the local newspaper, giving the names and addresses of the four men who had reported to the police after seeing the ghost and hearing the scream, the night Bob and Pete had been at the mansion.

He picked the address farthest away from the old mansion, and got there just as a car turned in the driveway and a man got out. It was one of the four men, a Mr. Charles Davis, and he answered Jupiter's questions readily.

He and a neighbor from across the street had been sitting in his patio, smoking and discussing baseball, when two men had walked by and called out to them. He hadn't recognized the men, but assumed they lived nearby in the development. They had suggested a walk up to look at the old Green mansion by moonlight before it was torn down, and one of them, a man with a deep voice, had been so persuasive that the two had joined them. He himself had taken two flashlights from his garage and given one to his friend.

Then the four of them had walked toward the Green mansion. On the way they had seen two more residents of the development and the man with the deep voice had talked them into joining the group. He'd made it seem rather a lark, to go visit a supposedly haunted house before it was torn down, and had laughingly suggested they might see the ghost.

"He actually said you might see the ghost?" Jupiter asked, and Mr. Davis nodded.

"Something like that," he said. "And as it turned out, we did. The whole thing was mighty peculiar, if you ask me."

"You didn't know the first two men?" Jupiter inquired.

"I thought I might have seen one of them," Mr. Davis told him. "The other was a stranger to me, but I judged he lived in the development someplace. We have lots of neighbors we don't know here. Most of us have only been here a year or so."

"How many of you were there when you reached the house?" Jupiter asked.

"Six," Mr. Davis told him. "Although somebody else said there were seven, I know there were only six of us when we started up the driveway. Of course, somebody could have followed us out of curiosity. After we heard the scream and then started to look inside, nobody thought much about counting. And it was mighty dark. After we left, we split up. My friend and I and our two neighbors decided we'd better notify the police. I don't know what happened to the others. I guess they just didn't want any publicity."

At that moment a small wire-haired terrier came dashing across the yard and leaped around Mr. Davis's legs, yapping a happy welcome.

"Down, boy, down!" the man laughed, and patted the dog, which subsided onto the lawn, where he stretched out, panting, and watched his master.

Jupiter remembered, from Bob's account, that one of the men at the Green mansion had had a dog. He ventured a question.

"Sure," Mr. Davis told him. "I had Domino here with me. I always take him for an evening walk, so I took him along."

Jupiter stared at the dog. The dog met his eye. His mouth open, panting, the dog seemed to be laughing at him as if it knew something Jupiter didn't. Jupiter scowled. Again an idea was trying to come to him, and couldn't quite make it.

He ventured a few more questions, but Mr. Davis could tell him nothing new, so Jupiter thanked him and remounted his bicycle.

He rode home, slowly now, thinking furiously. When he got back to the salvage yard, the big main gates were shut. The sun was setting—he had spent longer in his quest for information than he had realized.

Jupiter found Konrad comfortably smoking a pipe in his little cottage.

"Hi-yup, Jupe," Konrad said as Jupiter entered. "You look like you're thinking so hard you pretty close to busting."

"Konrad," Jupiter said, hardly noticing the remark, "last night you heard me yell."

"Sure did," Konrad agreed. "Sounded like stuck pig, Jupe, hope you don't mind if I say it."

"I was trying to sound as hurt as I could," Jupiter told him. "But you wouldn't have heard me if my window and your window hadn't been open, would you?"

"Don't think so. What you getting at?"

Jupiter's face turned pink with sudden excitement. The scream that everyone had heard—and the dog! The dog that had seemed to be able to tell him something. Suddenly he remembered that in a Sherlock Holmes story there had been a dog that had told Sherlock Holmes a lot, too! By not doing a thing!

He turned and hurried back to the cottage where he

lived. All of a sudden ideas were tumbling in his mind and taking form.

The policeman at the Green mansion hadn't been able to hear him yell, not when he was inside with the door shut. But outside—yes, he'd heard him clearly! That was very significant!

Once inside the house, Jupiter got out the tape recorder and prepared to play the scream again, and along with it the bits of conversation Bob had recorded. He played it all through once, then sat very still for several minutes. He recalled exactly what Bob had told him the previous night. It all fitted! It had to fit!

The scream—the fact that no one was sure whether six or seven men had been in the house—even the dog! Now he knew what the dog might have told him if it could speak. There were a lot of other things he still didn't know, but he knew that much, he felt sure.

It was dark in the room, but he didn't bother to turn on the light as he grabbed up the telephone and put through a person-to-person call for Bob Andrews in Verdant Valley. After a long delay, it was Miss Green herself who answered the phone.

"Is this Bob's friend, Jupiter Jones?" she asked, and her voice seemed to tremble.

"Yes, Miss Green," Jupiter answered. "I wanted to talk to Bob. I believe I have some ideas and——"

But her voice stopped him.

"Bob isn't here," she said, sounding very distracted.

"Neither is his friend Pete. My great-nephew Chang is missing, too. All three of them have just—just disappeared!"

CHAPTER 8

Runaway!

The morning after his telephone call to Jupiter—the same morning Jupiter was so busy at the salvage yard—Bob, together with Pete and Chang, was exploring Verdant Valley on horseback. None of the three boys had any notion of the dangerous and exciting events that were ahead of them that day.

They weren't planning anything more exciting at the moment than a look at the caves which the 3-V Winery used as aging cellars in which to store the wine made from the grapes grown in Verdant Valley. These caves, as Chang explained, were really old mines, most of them dug into the high ridge to the west of the valley long before.

Mostly, the boys' plan was to stay away from the house for the day. They couldn't very well investigate the theft of the Ghost Pearls, because if Sheriff Bixby was correct, and city thieves had taken them, thieves and pearls both were probably back in San Francisco by now.

But the big house was swarming with reporters, brought there by the news of the appearance of the ghost and the theft of the pearls. And Miss Lydia Green, whom they had seen only briefly, looking very haggard and worn, had asked them not to give the reporters the chance to guess that Pete and Bob were the boys who had seen the first ghostly manifestation at the empty house in Rocky Beach. She was afraid this would just make the reporters write bigger and more sensational stories, speculating about the ghost and why the boys had come. As she said, the stories were going to do enough damage anyway.

So Bob, Pete and Chang had eaten breakfast in the kitchen and had quietly slipped away to the stables, where they had saddled three horses. Chang did most of the work, for Bob and Pete had only had limited experience with horses while visiting dude ranches.

Now, flashlights clipped to their belts for use later in exploring the wine caves—or mines—they rode slowly through the cultivated fields, between the bushy grape vines, where purple grapes were ripening fast in the hot sun.

Chang was visibly gloomy.

"There should be at least a hundred pickers in the fields now," he told them. "And several trucks carrying the grapes they picked to the pressing houses. But look. You can hardly see a dozen people picking. And only one truck. The others have all left for fear of the ghost. If this keeps up, Aunt Lydia and the vineyard will be ruined. She'll never be able to pay off the notes, and they will be due very soon."

Bob and Pete couldn't think of anything to say to cheer him up, but Pete tried.

"Our partner, Jupiter Jones, is working on the mystery of the ghost right this minute, back in Rocky Beach," he said. "Jupe is pretty brainy. If he can solve the mystery and quiet down the ghost somehow, maybe the pickers will come back."

"Only if it happens very soon," Chang said. "Otherwise the pickers will go elsewhere. This morning old Li told me that I am the one causing such ill-fortune to Verdant Valley. She said I brought bad luck with me when I came from Hong Kong a year and a half ago and that I should go back."

"That's silly," Bob said promptly. "How could you bring bad luck?"

Chang shook his head. "I do not know. But it is true that since I have been here, there have been many misfortunes. Batches of wine have spoiled, casks have leaked, machinery has broken down time and time again. Nothing has gone right."

"I don't see how anybody can blame you for that!" Pete declared.

"Perhaps it is true, though," Chang said. "Perhaps if I

83

were to go back to Hong Kong, the ghost would go with me and fortune would smile again on Verdant Valley. If I could be sure that was the case, I would go tomorrow. Not for anything would I bring trouble and misfortune to my honored great-aunt!"

Chang seemed so gloomy, Bob decided it was time to change the subject.

"You call Miss Green your aunt, and Mr. Carlson your uncle," he said. "I haven't been able to figure out the actual relationship. Old Mathias Green was your grandfather——"

"My great-grandfather," Chang said. "Miss Green is really my great-aunt, but I call her aunt by courtesy. Uncle Harold is a distant cousin of hers. I don't know the exact relationship, but I call him uncle also, by courtesy. We three are the only members of this branch of the family."

Pete looked ahead, down the long, narrow valley, walled on both sides by steep mountain ridges. As far as he could see, grape vines grew.

"So this place is really all yours, Chang?" he asked with interest. "I mean, as the only direct descendant of old Mathias."

"Oh, no, no," the other boy said. "It belongs to Aunt Lydia. Her mother started it and Aunt Lydia has worked all her life to build it up.

"She wants to deed it to me, but I will not permit it. So she is leaving it to me in her will. I have decided that then I will give half of it to Uncle Harold. After all, he has worked hard as Aunt Lydia's business manager to make the vineyard and the winery prosper. Only——" he looked gloomy again "——if the vineyard and the winery are lost because there is no money to pay off the loans, none of us will have anything."

A jeep came down the dirt road toward them. They pulled to a stop to let it pass. Chang was riding a big black colt named Ebony, full of life and spirit, which he had to hold in tightly. Pete was riding a young mare, Nellie, who was a bit nervous, and he, too, had to keep her under tight control. Bob was on an older mare, called Rockingchair, because of her easy motion and placid disposition.

The jeep stopped. Mr. Jensen leaned out.

"Hi, Chang," he said. "I suppose you see how few pickers we have this morning?"

The boy nodded.

"Those varmints last night did their work well," Jensen continued. "Every time they told about the ghost they claimed to see, they made it bigger and uglier, until at last it was breathing smoke and flames. They scared the daylights out of the other pickers. I've sent out word for help, but I'm afraid we won't get it."

He shook his head.

"I'm on the way up to report to Miss Green," he said. "It doesn't look good."

The jeep roared off. The boys started their horses walking again and with an effort Chang threw off his gloomy mood.

"What can't be helped, can't be helped," he said. "There's nothing we can do, so let's try to enjoy ourselves."

They rode the length of the valley, stopping now and then, while Chang showed the other pressing houses. Some time after noon they began to get hot and hungry. They had sandwiches and canteens with them, and feed for the horses in their saddle bags.

"I know where we can be cool and comfortable," Chang told them. He led them past an old building, the old grape-pressing house, now only used at rush periods. They rode a few hundred yards farther, and they were in the shadow of the western ridge of the valley wall. Around an out-cropping of rock they found a small, shaded space where they dismounted, tied up their horses and gave them the grain they had brought.

Then Chang led them around the other side of the rocky outcropping and they found themselves outside a heavy door set into the rock wall of the ridge.

"This is one of the entrances to the aging caves, or mines, I told you about," Chang said. He pulled the door open with an effort. Beyond it was a shaft of darkness that ran straight into the ridge. "We'll explore this after we eat."

He reached for a switch inside the door and clicked it, but nothing happened.

"Darn," he said. "I forgot. The dynamos aren't on. We have to make our own electricity here, and the dynamos for different sections are only turned on when there's work being done inside. Oh well, we can use our flashlights."

He unbuckled his own light and shone it forward. Pete and Bob saw a long corridor, rock walled, with timbers overhead supporting the roof. On each side of the corridor was a long row of large casks, bigger than water barrels, lying on their sides. Down the middle of the corridor ran two narrow rails, and a small flatcar stood a few feet away.

"The casks can be put on that flatcar and rolled down here to the entrance," Chang explained. "If we want to ship a whole cask, we just load it onto a truck that backs up to the entrance. That way the heavy casks are pretty easy to handle.

"Well, suppose we sit here inside the door and eat, and take it easy for a while."

Pete and Bob were delighted to flop down beside him with their backs against the stone, and start in on the lunch. It was cool inside, though the heat of the afternoon was only a few feet away.

As they ate, they could look out at the valley. The old pressing house was in their line of vision, but no one, looking in their direction, could see them inside the cave.

They finished eating and talked for awhile, enjoying the coolness. Chang was telling them about his life in Hong Kong, where he had always been surrounded by people, in contrast to the quiet life in Verdant Valley, when the boys saw several old cars pull up outside the pressing house a few hundred yards away.

Half a dozen men, all of them big and powerful looking, got out and stood in a little group. They seemed to be waiting for something.

Chang broke off what he was saying, and frowned.

"I wonder why they aren't busy picking?" he asked aloud. "Today we need every hand available."

A moment later, Mr. Jensen's jeep drove up and they saw the burly man get out. He went inside the old pressing house. The men followed him and the door shut.

"I suppose Mr. Jensen is going to work on the machinery," Chang murmured. "Since the pressing house isn't being used today. Well, it's his business, I don't like him very well, but I have to admit he knows how to handle the workers, even though he does get rather rough with them at times."

He leaned on an elbow and turned to Bob and Pete.

"Want to explore the aging tunnels now?" he asked.

They agreed and unsnapped the flashlights from their belts. Pete stood up and as he did so, slipped. His hand shot out to steady himself. The flashlight seemed to zip from between his fingers and fell on the rock with a tinkle of broken glass. When he picked it up, the lens and bulb were both broken.

"Darn!" Pete said, disgusted with himself. "Now I haven't got a flashlight."

"We could get by with just two," Chang said, "but——"

He was gazing at the jeep parked outside the pressing house.

"I have it," he said. "Borrow Mr. Jensen's. The one he loaned me last night. He carries it in the toolbox with the other gear during the day. We'll get it back to him long before dark. I'll ride over and get it."

But Pete insisted that as he had broken his flashlight, it was up to him to do the chore of getting the replacement. Chang wrote out a note, to leave in the toolbox, telling Mr. Jensen that they had borrowed the flashlight and would return it later.

"When he's busy he hates to be interrupted," he said. "Besides, the flashlight actually belongs to Aunt Lydia, so he won't mind our using it for a while."

Pete got on his horse and started trotting across the field toward the pressing house. In a couple of minutes he reined up beside the parked jeep. His horse, having rested, was feeling frisky, and he had to hold the reins tightly to keep it from bolting away.

With one hand, he flipped open the toolbox of the jeep and saw inside a jumble of tools. The flashlight was not in sight. Then he saw it, tucked well down into a corner. He pulled it out and slipped it inside his belt. It was an old-fashioned flashlight, with a large, black fiber barrel, and had no ring that he could use to hang it to his belt clip.

He dropped the note Chang had given him into the toolbox and left the box open so Mr. Jensen would be sure to see it. Then, with some difficulty, he remounted and started trotting back to where Bob and Chang waited.

He had covered a hundred yards when he heard a voice shouting behind him. Pete looked back. Mr. Jensen was standing beside his jeep, shouting at him. Pete held up the flashlight, then pointed to the jeep, to indicate that the note explained everything, and kept on trotting.

A moment later the man leaped into the jeep, while the other men who had been in the building with him crowded outside to watch, and raced the sturdy vehicle across the field, between the grapevines, after Pete.

Obviously, he wanted Pete to stop. Wondering at the man's excitement, Pete reined in his horse, which danced a little.

"Steady, girl, steady!" he said soothingly.

But the horse, eyeing the approaching jeep, still side-stepped nervously.

The jeep roared up and stopped. Mr. Jensen practically catapulted out of it and ran toward Pete.

"You young thief!" he roared. "I'll tan your hide! I'll teach you to——"

The rest of what he had to say was lost.

As he came closer, the nervous horse under Pete gave a great leap. Then, before Pete could get himself set, it bolted.

At a dead run it started tearing down the vineyard, angling toward the mountain slope, and Pete could do nothing to stop it.

Knees pressed tightly against the horse and unashamedly clutching the pommel of the Western type saddle, Pete hung on for dear life.

CHAPTER 9

A Desperate Flight

The mare thundered along between the rows of grape-vines, heading straight for the rocky ridge of the western wall of the valley. Pete, unable to do anything but hang on, saw that there was a trail slanting up the slope, narrow but not too steep.

The frightened horse automatically selected the trail and continued galloping upward. Pete hoped the slope would slow her down, and it did, but only enough to let him get set better so that he was in less danger of tumbling out of the saddle.

He risked turning his head to look back. Mr. Jensen had jumped back into his jeep and was chasing him. The little car, driven pell-mell across the fields, pulled up to a stop where the narrow trail up the slope began. Jensen leaped out and shook his fist after Pete.

Then Pete saw Bob and Chang. As soon as his mare bolted they must have run to their horses, mounted, and set out after him. They swerved around Mr. Jensen and the jeep and came up the trail behind Pete. Chang, on his big black stallion, Ebony, was in the lead, urging the animal on and gaining on Pete.

Bob, on the slower Rockingchair, was behind and losing ground.

A sudden swerve by Nellie as she went around a rocky outcropping nearly unseated Pete. He grabbed the pommel tightly and held on again. Coming to a short level stretch, the nervous mare picked up speed.

Then Pete heard pounding hooves behind him. Chang pulled up daringly beside him on the narrow trail, reached out and grabbed Nellie's reins just behind the bit.

Chang slowed Ebony, meanwhile holding tight to Nellie's reins and forcing the mare to slow. Almost as if she had made up her mind to stop running anyway, Nellie stopped. Ebony stopped beside her and both horses, their flanks wet with sweat, heaved deeply for breath.

"Golly, Chang, thanks," Pete said with fervor. "This horse acted as if she wanted to run right over the mountain."

Chang was staring at him with a peculiar look.

"What is it, Chang? Did I do something wrong?"

"I was just thinking," Chang said. "Why did Jensen make your horse bolt?"

"He wasn't trying to," Pete answered. "He was yelling at me. Calling me a thief. He was pretty angry."

"When I passed him," Chang said, "his face was twisted like the mask of an evil spirit. He was in a mindless fury. In his pocket he carries a revolver—to kill rattlesnakes that are found among the rocks—and he half drew it as if he was going to shoot at you."

"It beats me," Pete said, scratching his head. "Why should he get so upset because I borrowed a worthless old flashlight like this one?"

He pulled the old, fiber-cased flashlight from his belt and held it up. Chang stared at it.

"That's not Jensen's flashlight!" he exclaimed. "I mean it isn't the one he usually carries in the jeep, the one he loaned me last night."

"Well, it was in the toolbox," Pete told him. "It was the only one, so I took it because you said it was okay."

"Looks as if I was wrong," Chang muttered. "Pete, may I please see the flashlight?"

"Why, sure." Pete passed it over and Chang held it in his hand, weighing it.

"It is very light," he said. "It does not feel as if it has any batteries in it."

"Then it's useless," Pete said in disgust. "Why should Mr. Jensen get so riled up over a worthless flashlight?"

"Perhaps——" Chang began. At that moment Bob caught up with them. He was breathless, more from excitement than anything else. His old mare had decided she didn't want to run uphill and had slowed to a walk.

"Here you are!" he said in relief. Then he noticed their expressions. "What is it?" he asked. "Something wrong?"

"We are going to see what made Jensen so angry," Chang told him in a quiet voice. He unscrewed the base of the flashlight. Then he reached in and pulled out a wad of tissue paper. As Pete and Bob watched, he carefully unfolded the tissue paper. Something was coiled up inside. He uncoiled it and held it up in the sunlight. It swayed in his hand.

"The Ghost Pearls!" Pete shouted.

"Mr. Jensen stole them!" Bob yelled.

Chang's lips were set tightly.

"Yes, apparently Jensen stole them, or, more likely, had two of the men who work for him steal them," he said. "He had them hidden in this old flashlight, in his toolbox, all along. What better place of concealment? A flashlight is just the right size to hold them, and it doesn't look suspicious, especially if it is in among some old tools. He could just drive right out of the valley with the pearls, and never have to risk taking them from some other hiding place."

"It was a good hiding place, all right," Bob agreed. "He couldn't figure that we'd need a flashlight.

"No. He couldn't see us, and no one else was around. He had no reason to think anyone would come along while he was in the pressing house," Chang said. "I wonder what he was doing in there with those men? Plotting

95

something, perhaps. Indeed, I begin to wonder many things. One of them is whether Jensen does not know more than he has told us about the accidents, the wine spoilage, and other incidents in recent months."

"Say," Pete interjected, "hadn't we better get back to the house with these pearls, tell Mr. Carlson and your aunt, and get the sheriff after Jensen?"

"It may not be that simple," Chang said slowly. "Jensen is a dangerous man, and can be very brutal and reckless. He will not let us reveal his guilt without trying to stop us."

"What can he do?" Bob asked anxiously.

"I think we'd better have a look first," Chang told him and slipped off Ebony. "Bob, you stay here and hold the horses. Pete, you and I will go down the trail until we can see back down into the valley."

The two boys gave Bob their reins. Then together they eased down the trail toward the rocky projection that hid the valley.

Crouched low, they peered around the rocks. Now they could see the valley below. Two men stood at the foot of the trail up the slope, as if on guard. Bob and Chang could see the jeep bouncing swiftly toward the tiny village at the end of the valley. Then they saw the two cars that had been parked by the old pressing house swaying and bumping over the cultivated ground. These were maneuvered up to the trail. One drove several yards up the trail, effectively blocking it to a horse, and the other was parked across the trail behind it as an additional barrier.

Chang drew in his breath.

"Jensen is going for horses!" he said. "He's had his men block the trail so we can't ride down and gallop past them. If we do ride back down, we'll have to dismount to get past those cars, and they can grab us."

"You mean he has us trapped?" Pete asked.

"He thinks he has. We can't go back. If we go forward, across the ridge and down the other side, we come out into Hashknife Canyon. It's a very rugged box canyon. That is, at one end there is no way out. At the other end there is a trail, which becomes a rough road that eventually joins up with the main road to San Francisco.

"If we take that trail, Jensen will easily follow us. Also, he will send men in cars to block the other end of the trail. He plans to capture us and take the pearls back."

"He can't get away with it!" Pete exclaimed. "Even if he does get the pearls, we'll tell someone."

"I'm sure he's thought of that." Chang's quiet tone made a shiver go down Pete's spine. "And he will see to it that we can't tell anyone—ever. Remember, all those men are his accomplices. No one else knows what happened."

Pete understood. He swallowed hard.

"Come on!" Chang said abruptly, pulling Pete back. He was grinning now, his black eyes shining with excitement.

"I have an idea!" he exclaimed. "Jensen will need time to get to the village, get horses, and get back here. He

97

thinks he has us bottled up. But we'll fool him. We have to hurry, though."

They ran back to their horses, where Bob was waiting impatiently, and remounted.

"Well?" Bob asked. "What's happening?"

"Jensen has us cut off," Pete said. "He wants the pearls back and he doesn't care what he does to get them. Apparently all those men we saw are working with him."

"But I have a plan to make him look foolish!" Chang said jubilantly. "We have to ride over the ridge—this trail leads to a pass—and down into the canyon beyond. I'll lead the way."

He urged Ebony up the trail and the big stallion set a fast pace. Chang made all the speed possible without exhausting the horses. Bob came second, with Pete behind him. Bob's slower mare, obviously disliking all this activity, was kept moving by the nervous mare at her heels.

In half an hour they reached the top of the pass, and could see down into the canyon beyond. It looked rugged and narrow and desolate.

Chang paused only for a moment, then started Ebony on the down trail. The going was easier on this side, and in half an hour they reined their panting horses in on the rocky floor of the canyon.

"The trail out of Hashknife Canyon goes that way." Chang pointed. "It becomes a road that, as I said, joins the main road in a few miles. Jensen will expect us to head that way. So we're heading in just the opposite direction."

He turned Ebony, and the horse started picking its way along through the rocks, between the narrow cliff walls.

"Now we have to look for two yellow rocks, about twenty feet above the floor of the canyon," Chang called to them. "One rock is just above the other."

They rode on for ten minutes, then Pete, who had very keen eyesight, spotted the rocks.

"There they are!" he pointed. Chang nodded. At a point directly below the two yellow rocks he dismounted.

"We get off here," he said. Pete and Bob dismounted. Unexpectedly, Chang slapped all three horses on the rump. Ebony, startled, bolted away down the canyon and the others followed.

"From here we go on foot," Chang explained. "And on our knees and stomachs, too. There's a small pool of water at the closed end of the canyon. The horses will smell it and head for it to drink. When Jensen realizes we've given him the slip and comes back to hunt in this canyon, he'll find them, but that'll be hours away."

He looked up. "There used to be a trail here," he said. "Rock slides took most of it away—luckily for us. But we can climb it. We have to get on the top of that first yellow rock."

He started up, finding rocky toeholds. Bob followed him. Pete was behind Bob and gave him a helping hand when necessary. In a couple of minutes they stood on top of the yellow rock. Bob and Pete were startled to see an

99

opening in the cliff. The second yellow rock overhung it, like a roof, and hid it from sight from below.

"A cave," Chang said. "Many years ago a miner found a rich lode inside, so he started tunneling, using the cave as the mouth of his mine. This is where we're going. Quickly, before Jensen or his men have a chance to spot us."

He ducked into the cave. Bob and Pete followed him into the darkness without the slightest idea of where they were going or what would come next.

CHAPTER 10

Captured!

Chang led them to the rear of the cave, which seemed quite large once they were inside. Then Chang's light showed them the mouth of a tunnel—an old mine gallery, really, dug many years before. Old timbers were still in place, bracing the roof, though some rocks had fallen to the floor.

"I'll tell you my plan," Chang said. "There's a whole network of mine galleries under this ridge. When I first came to this country, the old mines fascinated me. There was an old fellow named Dan Duncan, a little shriveled old man who'd spent his whole life scratching tiny bits of gold out of the old mines.

"He knew them like you know the streets of your home town. He's sick in a hospital now, but before he got sick, he showed me through these old mines. And if you know exactly how to go, there's a way from this cave all the way through to the wine cellars on the other side of the ridge."

"Golly!" Pete exclaimed. "You mean we're going back through the mines while Jensen and his men are looking for us outside?"

"That's it," Chang agreed. "Many of the workers must be in league with Jensen. But this way we'll come out only a mile from the house and be there with our story before anyone can stop us. There are two pretty tricky spots where only a boy or a very small man can squeeze through, but they were passable last time I tried it six months ago."

Bob gulped slightly. They seemed a long way underground, and the darkness was awfully black. He put his hand in his pocket, and his fingers touched his piece of green chalk.

"Shouldn't we mark our trail in?" he asked. "Then if we did get lost, we could find our way back."

"We won't get lost," Chang said. "And if Jensen found the marks he could follow us without any trouble."

He seemed very confident of himself, but Bob knew that you can get lost when you least expect it. So did Pete.

"Listen," Pete said. "Our secret mark is a question mark. Suppose we mark our trail with question marks, but put up arrows, too, leading in different directions. Then only we know for sure which marks indicate the real trail. Anyone who came after us would lose a lot of time following the fake marks."

Chang approved of this.

"Anyway," he said, Jensen doesn't know about this mine or the fact that it connects with the wine cellars. But you're right, we could get lost ourselves. However, we won't mark the entrance. That would be a giveaway. We'll start the marking once we're inside the gallery."

With that they started into the old mine diggings. The way was narrow, and at times the roof was low. Occasionally they came across intersecting or branching galleries, where miners years before had followed a wandering vein of ore in the rock. Bob marked the proper route with question marks. He also drew bold arrows pointing down the wrong galleries. The trail he left would have confused anyone who didn't know the secret.

But presently they came to a spot where the gallery ahead had partly caved in. Rocks and dirt on the floor almost closed the passage. Chang called a halt.

"We have to crawl now," he said. "I'll go first."

He pulled something from his waist and handed it to Pete.

"Here's the old flashlight with the pearls," he said. "You take care of them, Pete. They'll be in my way if I have to dig."

"Sure, Chang," Pete agreed. He thrust the old flashlight with its precious contents inside his belt and buckled the belt tight so the flashlight couldn't slip. "I certainly wish I had a real light, though."

"That's a problem." Chang considered a moment. "We only have two lights. Look, Bob, suppose you let Pete have your light? I'll go first, with my light. You follow me. Pete will follow you. That way we'll all have light, because the light behind you will shine ahead and show you your way, too."

The idea didn't appeal to Bob much. Down there in the pitch blackness the flashlight was something nice and solid and bright to hang on to.

However, Chang's idea was sensible, so he passed his flashlight to Pete. As it happened, being rid of the flashlight helped him crawl better, which was good because the leg which had recently had the brace on it was beginning to feel quite tired.

The caved-in section was only a hundred yards long, but it seemed as if they would never get through it. Ahead of Bob, Chang at times lay flat on his stomach and pulled himself along. Then Bob followed. Behind him, Pete, his light shining up to assist Bob, repeated the process. Like inch-worms they moved ahead. Several times Chang paused to dig a wider opening or to push small rocks to one side.

Once Bob brushed against the roof and a small rock fell on his back and wedged him there so he could not move in either direction. He had to fight a feeling of panic while Pete crawled up behind him and, lying on his legs, reached up and wiggled the rock loose.

"Thanks, Pete," Bob gasped. Then he wriggled on. Behind him, Pete, who was bigger, stopped to scoop out a little dirt so he could get through without having the same thing happen to him.

Bob was panting for breath when they finally crawled out into a place where they could sprawl out full length with their backs against the rock wall.

Overhead, the lights showed the old timbers, used to brace the roof, bulging downward under the weight above them. But they had held all these years so there was no use thinking that they would suddenly break now.

For a while they just lay there, getting their breath back. Then Chang spoke.

"That's the worst," he said. "There's one more bad spot, but not as bad as that. One thing is sure"—he chuckled—"Jensen can never follow us through here. He's too big."

As they rested, Chang told them something of the history of the network of mine tunnels they were finding their way through. The mines had first been worked around 1849, when gold was discovered in California. After the first rich gold was gone, many miners moved on, but some stayed, working hard, digging into the mountain for the gold that wandered in thin veins through the rock. Little by little the mines had been extended.

The valley, however, had depended on its grapevines and the wine it made, and after the death of old Mathias Green, Miss Lydia Green's mother had been able to buy it and start building up the vineyard and winery. But then, in 1919, had come Prohibition, when it was illegal to sell wine or any kind of alcoholic beverage.

The vineyard had almost collapsed then. But the workers, with nothing else to do, had turned gold miners, and tunneled deeper and deeper searching for the elusive metal. The next hardship had been the Depression, beginning late in 1929, when no one had any money, and the gold mining had been pressed frantically by every able-bodied man in the region as one source of cash.

When things began to get better, around 1940, the gold mining was abandoned. By then Prohibition had been repealed and the vineyard was flourishing again. But all that digging for so many years had left quite a network of abandoned mines and tunnels under the mountain ridge.

"Is there any gold now?" Bob asked eagerly.

"A little, but it would take a pickaxe and probably dynamite to get it," Chang told them. "Well, let's get going. It must be pretty late by now. Aunt Lydia will be worrying."

Bob kept marking their trail with question marks, mixed with fake arrows, as they went. Only once did Chang seem puzzled, at a point where three galleries stretched away from the same point. He finally picked the right-hand one, but it ended in a cave-in after about three hundred yards.

"Wrong way," he said and pointed his light at the tunnel floor. "Look."

They looked. White bones gleamed in the light. For a startled moment Bob and Pete thought it was a human skeleton. Then they saw the bones belonged to some animal who had been caught by the roof cave-in.

"A burro. Some miner was using it to move ore out," Chang said. "Lucky he wasn't caught himself. Or maybe he was. Nobody has ever dug in there to see."

Bob glanced down at the white skull of the burro and shivered a little. He was glad to hurry after Chang as the other boy led them away.

After selecting the right passage, Chang seemed to have no trouble. He led them rapidly past many branching passages, until he stopped so abruptly Bob bumped into him.

"We've come to The Throat," he explained.

"The Throat?" Pete asked. "What's that?"

"It's a natural rock fault that goes through to the mines on the other side of the ridge," Chang said. "But it's pretty rough and narrow."

He shone his light into a passageway that seemed to be a mere slit in the rock. Just high enough for a boy to stand erect, it was too narrow for him to enter, unless he slipped in sidewise.

"That's it, Chang said, reading their thoughts. "We have to ease through sidewise."

"Are you—are you sure it goes through?" Bob asked. The longer he stayed down here underground, the less he liked it. And the idea of easing through that narrow slit did not appeal to him in the least.

"Sure," Chang said. "I've been through it. Besides, feel the air current? There's air coming from that side."

It was true. They could feel the air on their cheeks.

"We've got to get through," Chang said. "It's the only connection between the two sides of the mountain, and only a boy or a small man can make it. I just hope I haven't grown too much in the last six months! Well, I'll go first. You two wait until I'm all the way through. Then I'll flash my light three times, and you, Bob, follow. Pete and I will shine our lights in from each end to help you see. When Bob is through, I'll flash my light three times more and you come, Pete."

They agreed. Chang slipped into The Throat, holding his light in his right hand. Carefully he began to sidestep his way along, making no sudden movement that might get him jammed in the narrow, uneven space.

Pete and Bob, watching, saw his light move jerkily along, his body hiding it most of the time. Chang had said that once through The Throat, they were almost to the section where the wine casks were stored for aging, and would be back at the house in an hour.

Chang actually made pretty good speed, but to the two boys waiting it seemed forever before they saw three spaced flashes of light announcing he had got through.

"Okay, Bob," Pete said, "It'll be easy for you, you're smaller than either of us."

"Sure," Bob said, his throat somewhat dry, "It'll be a

cinch. Just give me some light."

He slid sideways into The Throat. Pete shone his light after him, holding it close to the floor, and from the other end came a faint gleam which was Chang's flashlight.

Pete watched his friend move away slowly. Presently Bob's body, filling most of The Throat, cut off the light from the other end. Pete kept his light on a little longer, then, figuring Bob must be much closer to Chang now, shut it off.

He waited tensely for the three flashes of light that would be the signal for him to start. For some reason they were delayed.

Then he heard a faint yell, followed by words. "Pete! Don't——"

It was Chang's voice, muffled by the narrow Throat. And it sounded as if it had been cut off abruptly, maybe by a hand over his mouth.

Pete could guess, though, what Chang had been trying to say. *Don't come!*

He waited for some other sound or signal. Presently he saw the light flash three times. Then, after a pause, three times more.

But the flashes were jerky and were shorter than Chang had made them.

Pete knew they were a trap. Someone else—not Chang or Bob—was signaling him to come through The Throat.

That, and the yell, gave him a pretty good idea of what had happened. Chang and Bob had been captured!

CHAPTER 11

A Fortune in a Skull

Back at Rocky Beach, at just about this same moment, Jupiter Jones was talking on the telephone with Miss Lydia Green. "Bob and Pete and Chang have *disappeared?*"

"They're just *gone!*" The woman's voice sounded terribly distressed. "They started out on horseback, to explore the valley, and said they'd be gone all day. We were so terribly busy here, with the sheriff and reporters and everything, that we didn't miss them until supper.

"Then we discovered they weren't anyplace in the valley. We haven't even found their horses yet."

For once Jupiter's mental machinery wouldn't seem to work. All he could do was say helplessly, "But where could they be?"

"We think they're in the mines," Miss Green told him.

111

"There's a network of old mines under the mountain here, and we use part of it for a wine cellar in which to age our wines. We believe Chang may have taken them in there to explore, and we have men starting now to search the mines and look for them."

Jupiter pinched his lip. His mental gears were starting to revolve. The Ghost Pearls had disappeared. Now his partners and Chang had disappeared. There might not be a connection but he suspected there was.

He thought as fast as he could. This was an emergency and emergency measures were called for.

"You have all of the men available looking for them?" he asked.

"Of course," Miss Green told him. "All the field workers—those who haven't deserted us—and the winery workers, and even the household staff. We're exploring the mines where the wine casks are. We've also sent men out into the desert beyond Verdant Valley to see if the boys could have ridden out there."

"Tell them to look for question marks," Jupiter said. Knowing his two partners, he knew that wherever they were, they'd try to leave the mark of The Three Investigators somehow.

"Question marks?" Miss Green sounded puzzled.

"Interrogation marks," Jupiter said. "Probably drawn in chalk. If anyone finds a question mark, or several question marks, have him report it immediately."

"But I don't understand!" Miss Green said helplessly.

"I can't explain over the telephone. I'm coming up there right away. Can you have a car meet us at the airport? I'll bring someone with me—Bob Andrew's father. I know he'll come."

"Yes—yes." The woman's voice fluttered. "Of course. Oh, I do hope they haven't been hurt."

Jupiter thanked her and hung up. Then he called Bob's father, who, after his first astonishment, arranged to meet him at the airport, and hung up again. Jupiter hurried out to tell Konrad to take care of the salvage yard next day the best he could, and right now to drive him to the airport in the salvage yard's smaller truck.

Jupiter was on the job, but what he could do remained very uncertain. He doubted that Bob and Pete and Chang were merely lost in the mines and would be found so easily.

Nor was he wrong. A short time later, Bob and Chang were whisked through the ring of men searching the mines on the Verdant Valley side of the ridge, and driven away totally unseen and unsuspected. They were unseen because they were inside large wine casks, and wine casks were such common objects around the vineyard that no one gave them a second thought, even when they were loaded on a truck and driven away.

So, even as they were being hunted, Bob and Chang were on their way in the hands of their captor, Mr. Jensen, to an unknown destination. And Pete, bearer of the fabulously valuable Ghost Pearls, was wandering through the

complex network of mine galleries, on the other side of
The Throat, where no one was searching because no
one—except Jensen and his henchmen—knew either that
the boys had ridden over the ridge into Hashknife Canyon, or that there was a way from the mines on that side
into the area where the wine casks were stored.

Pete, as soon as he realized that Bob and Chang must
have been caught by someone waiting for them at the
other end of The Throat, backed away in the darkness
and watched intently. He was looking for a sign that
someone was coming through The Throat after him.

But no light appeared. Pete guessed that whoever had
caught his friends were men, too big to risk getting stuck
in The Throat. That meant they wouldn't be coming after
him, at least not unless they could round up someone
small enough to slip through the narrow crevice in the
rock.

As he couldn't stay in there and wait, his only hope
was to retrace his path, back into Hashknife Canyon, and
then hide among the rocks there until next morning.
There were sure to be men hunting for them by then, and
he could help Bob and Chang best by staying free until
he could tell all he knew.

He made sure the old flashlight holding the Ghost
Pearls was still fast under his belt. Then, saying a silent
prayer that his good flashlight would hold out, he started
back the way they had come.

Now Bob's insistence on marking their trail paid off. A

little hunting picked out one question mark after the other, chalked in green on the rocks. He ignored the arrows Bob had put up to mislead any possible pursuers.

Even so, he went astray once. When Chang had led them up the gallery which ended in a cave-in, Bob had marked it as if it were the right route, and Pete followed the marks. He was brought up short by the closed passage, blocked by tons of rock, and the white bones of the little burro that had perished when the cave-in happened.

As Pete turned to retrace his steps, a thought stopped him. Had he better keep the pearls? He might get caught. Then if he didn't have the pearls, at least Jensen wouldn't get them.

He thought fast. To hide the pearls under a rock could be risky. All rocks looked alike down here, and if he marked the rock, maybe with his own blue chalk, the mark might be found. If there was only something distinctive that no one would pay any attention to——

His light shone on the white skull of the burro. That was it! Something that seemed so natural that no one would pay any attention to it, yet that he could always find again.

It took him only a moment to slide the Ghost Pearls, in their tissue paper wrapping, out of the old flashlight. He stuffed them inside the hollow skull and put it back in place just as it had been. Now he could easily find the gems once more.

He started back to get on the right track again. As he

paused where the three galleries intersected, another thought occurred to him. There was no use lugging the empty, fiber-cased flashlight with him. Just why the thought came to him, he didn't know, but he decided to put some pebbles in it and hide it. He had some remote idea that it might come in handy as a decoy if he were captured.

He put a few pebbles in his handkerchief, stuffed it into the fiber case, then dropped the flashlight behind a rock. A few feet away he carelessly arranged some smaller rocks so that when viewed closely they made an arrow· indicating the large rock. That would help him identify the rock if the necessity ever arose.

With that done, Pete made more rapid progress backward until he came to the very low stretch where he and the others had had to crawl on their stomachs to get through.

By now he had been underground a great many hours, and he was starting to feel both hungry, and sick of the darkness. But he couldn't hurry. Hurry would get him wedged in, maybe forever. Slow and easy in a tight spot was the only way.

He shifted the flashlight in his belt around to the side, where it would be out of the way, got down on his knees, then his stomach, and started to inch his way along.

Once a small rock fell directly in front of him, almost hitting him. He had a terrible moment when he feared the whole section of roof was going to collapse. Under him, as he lay full length, he felt the tiniest quivering of the earth. He lay breathless, expecting everything to fall, but nothing else did. The tiny trembling ended. He reached forward and rolled the rock to one side.

Breathing hard with relief, Pete took several minutes to pull himself together. He had a pretty good idea what happened. Somewhere there had been a very small earthquake, of which this ridge had felt only a distant quiver.

As Pete, and everyone else living in California, knew, the famous San Andreas fault—a vast crack in the earth's rocky crust—runs down beneath western California. The San Andreas fault caused the famous San Francisco earthquake of 1906. It caused the great earthquake in Alaska in 1964, when the land in some places was lifted or sunk more than thirty feet. Every year it caused hundreds of tiny tremors, some so slight only instruments would record them.

What Pete had felt was only the slightest quiver of earth slipping somewhere along the great length of the famous fault line in the earth's rocky surface. Fortunately, a few minutes' uneasiness was all it caused him.

Elsewhere it had had bigger consequences, but he could have no knowledge of that.

Breathing hard, Pete negotiated the rest of the distance until he could stand erect. Then he made all the time he could, following Bob's trail back to the cave from which they had entered the mines.

The cave was empty. All was silent. Outside the cave

mouth the blackness of night was like a curtain.

Pete eased slowly through the cave, stopping after each step to listen. He heard nothing. He wasn't using his flashlight, so he could see the cave mouth only as a slightly lighter spot in the darkness.

Step by step he approached the cave mouth. Again he stopped to listen, and heard nothing. He moved outside, inch by inch, reassured that the cave entrance hadn't been found.

When he was fully outside, he stopped for a moment to try to adjust his vision to the faint starlight of the night.

That was when someone leaped from behind the rocks outside the entrance.

Strong arms grabbed him and a big hand went across his mouth.

CHAPTER 12

Meeting with Mr. Won

Bob and Chang were in a room. It was a room with solid plaster walls, no window, and only one door. The door was locked—they had tried it.

The two boys' clothes were very much the worse for wear from crawling around underground. However, most of the dirt had been brushed off, and they had washed.

They had also eaten. In fact, they were just finishing a large tray full of Chinese food that was strange to Bob, but delicious.

Until now they had been too hungry to talk much. Now, comfortably full, they relaxed.

"I wonder where we are?" Bob said. With his stomach full, it was hard to feel quite as worried as he had been for the past few hours.

"We are in an underground room in a large city. Probably San Francisco," Chang told him.

"How do you figure that?" Bob asked. "We had blindfolds on. We could be anyplace."

"I have felt the floor quiver as big trucks went by outside. Big trucks mean a big city. Chinese servants put us in here and brought us food. San Francisco has the biggest Chinatown in the United States. We are in a secret room in the home of some very wealthy Chinese person."

Bob shook his head. "How do you figure *that?*"

"The food. It was cooked in genuine Chinese style, and cooked superbly. Only a very fine cook could have cooked it. Only a rich man could afford such a chef."

"You and Jupiter Jones would get along great," Bob told him. "I wish you lived down in Rocky Beach so you could join The Three Investigators."

"I would like that," Chang said wistfully. "Verdant Valley is quite lonely. In Hong Kong, there were always many other people around, many boys to talk to and play with. Now—— But I shall be a man soon and I shall take charge of the vineyard and the winery as my honored aunt wishes me to." Then he added, after a moment, "If I am permitted to do so."

Bob knew what he meant. If they ever got out of this mess—whatever it was. Jupe had certainly been right about one thing—there was obviously a lot more to the mystery than just the appearance of a ghost at a deserted house.

122

The boys' thoughts were interrupted by the sound of the door opening. An elderly Chinese man, wearing the garments of old China, stood there.

"Come!" he said.

"Come where?" Chang asked boldly.

"Does a mouse ask where he goes when an eagle's claws seize him?" the man asked. "Come!"

Squaring his shoulders, Chang marched out the door. Bob, standing as straight as he could, followed.

They followed the old Chinese down a corridor and into a tiny elevator. The elevator took them far up and stopped before a red door. The old man slid back the elevator door, opened the red door, and pushed Bob.

"Go in!" he said. "Speak truth or the eagle will eat you."

They were alone in a large, circular room, hung with a multitude of red drapes on which beautiful scenes had been embroidered in gold thread. Bob could see dragons, Chinese temples, even willow trees that seemed to sway in the wind.

"You admire my draperies?" a voice that was thin and old but very clear spoke. "They are five hundred years of age."

They looked across the room and saw that they were not alone after all. An old man sat in a great carved armchair of black wood, thickly padded with soft cushions.

He wore flowing robes, like those worn by the ancient Chinese emperors. Bob had seen pictures of them in

books. His face was small, thin, yellow like a badly with-
ered pear, and he peered at them through plain gold-
rimmed spectacles.

"Advance," he said quietly. "Sit down, small ones who
have caused me so much trouble."

Bob and Chang crossed the room on rugs so thick they
seemed to sink into them. Two small stools were arranged
as if waiting for them. They sat down, staring in wonder
at the old man.

"You may call me Mr. Won," the ancient Chinese said
to them. "I am one hundred and seven years old."

Bob could believe that. He was certainly the oldest
looking man Bob had ever seen. Yet he did not seem
feeble.

Mr. Won looked at Chang. "Small cricket, the blood of
my nation flows in your veins also. I speak of the old
China, not of the China of today. Your family has had
much to do with the old China. Your great-grandfather
stole one of our princesses for a bride. Of that I do not
speak. Women follow their hearts. But your great-grandfather stole something else. Or bribed an official to steal
it for him, which is the same thing. A string of pearls!"

Mr. Won showed the first sign of excitement.

"A string of priceless pearls," he said. "For more than
fifty years their whereabouts were unknown. Now they
have reappeared. And I must have them."

He leaned forward slightly. His voice became stronger.

"Do you hear that, small mice? *I must have the pearls!*"

124

By now Bob was feeling extremely nervous, for he knew perfectly well they didn't have the pearls to give Mr. Won. He wondered how Chang felt. Sitting beside him, Chang spoke boldly.

"Oh venerable one," he said, "we do not have the pearls. They are in the possession of another. One who is fleet of foot and stout of heart has them, and he has escaped with them to return them to my aunt. Return us to my aunt and I will try to persuade her to sell them to you, That is, if the letter she received from someone who claims to be a relative of the bride of my great-grand-father does not turn out to be true."

"It is not true!" Mr. Won said sharply. "It was sent by another, whom I know, to confuse things, for he, too, wishes to buy the pearls. I am rich, but he is richer. He will buy them unless I get them first. Therefore—*I must have them.*"

Chang bowed his head.

"We are small mice," he said, "and we are helpless. Those who captured us did not capture our friend. He has the pearls. He has courage, he will escape."

"They bungled!" Mr. Won's fingers drummed on the arm of his teakwood chair. "They will pay for letting him escape!"

"They almost caught him," Chang replied. "Somehow they guessed my plan. They were waiting in silence as first I, then my friend, slipped through a narrow passage no man could travel. Then I heard a pebble roll. I swung my light, saw someone, and shouted to my friend just as Jensen and his men seized us. So my friend escaped. The passage was too narrow for Jensen or his henchmen to get through."

"They bungled!" Mr. Won said. "When Jensen telephoned me last night to say he had the pearls and would bring them to me tonight, I warned him there must be no slip-up. Now——"

He paused. A silvery bell sounded somewhere. Mr. Won reached beneath the cushions of his chair and to Bob's surprise he brought out a telephone. He placed it to his ear and listened. After a moment he put it away again.

"There has been a new development," he said. "Let us wait."

They waited in silence. The silence seemed to grow bigger and bigger to Bob, though he knew it was just his nerves. What was going to happen next? The day had been full of so many surprises that almost nothing could seem surprising now.

Yet what did happen, somehow, was the one thing he hadn't expected.

The red door opened.

Dirty and mussed up and looking very pale and stubborn, Pete Crenshaw walked into the room.

CHAPTER 13

"I Must Have the Pearls!"

"Pete!" Bob and Chang jumped to their feet. "Are you all right?"

"I'm hungry, mostly," Pete said. "Outside of that I'm okay, though my arm hurts where Jensen's men twisted it trying to make me tell him where I hid the Ghost Pearls."

"Then you did hide them?" Bob asked excitedly.

"You did not tell where. I am sure of that," Chang added.

"You bet I didn't," Pete said grimly. "They were wild. If they knew——"

"Careful!" Chang said. "One listens."

Pete was suddenly silent. For the first time he saw Mr. Won.

"You are not a small mouse," Mr. Won said, looking

at Chang. "You are a small dragon, cast in the same image as your great-grandfather." He paused, thinking. "Would you like to be my son?" he asked, nearly bowling the boys over with surprise.

"I am rich, but I am heavy of heart for I have no male offspring. I will adopt you, you will be my son, with my wealth you will become a very powerful man."

"I am honored, venerable one," Chang said politely. "But in my heart I fear two things."

"Name them," Mr. Won requested.

"The first is that you wish me to betray my friends and obtain the Ghost Pearls for you," said Chang.

Mr. Won nodded. "Of course," he said. "As my son-to-be, that would be your duty."

"The second fear," Chang said, "is that, though you mean the words now, you would forget them when you had the pearls. However, that is of no importance, for I do not betray my friends."

Mr. Won sighed. "If you had accepted," he said, "I would indeed have forgotten. Now I know that I would truly adopt you as my son if you were willing. But you are not willing. Yet, I must have the pearls. They mean life to me. And they mean life to you."

Mr. Won reached beneath the cushions. He brought out from some secret recess a tiny bottle, a thin crystal glass and a round object which he held on his palm.

"Approach and observe," he said.

Chang, Bob and Pete edged up close to him and stared

at the thing that rested on the shrunken, shriveled, claw-like hand.

It had a curious, dead gray color and might have been a badly made marble.

It was Chang who recognized it.

"It is a Ghost Pearl," he said.

"A foolish name for it," Mr. Won stated. He dropped the priceless pearl into the small bottle. In the liquid inside it fizzed and bubbled until it was all gone—dissolved.

"The true name for these pearls," Mr. Won said, as he poured the liquid from the bottle into the crystal glass, "is pearls of life."

He drank the liquid, draining the last tiny drop from the glass. Then he replaced glass and bottle in the secret place from which they had come.

"Small dragon of the blood of Mathias Green," he said, "and your friends. I shall tell you something only a few men know, and those who know it are either very wise, or very rich, or both. The world calls them Ghost Pearls. The world knows they are priceless. Yet why are they priceless? Not because they are beautiful—as pearls, they are ugly. They look, if I may say so, dead. Is that not true?"

Not having any idea what Mr. Won was leading up to, the boys nodded. The man continued.

"For centuries a few, a very few, have been found at one spot in the Indian Ocean. Now, for some reason, no more can be found. Barely half a dozen strings of Ghost

Pearls—I use your name for them—exist in the world. They are treasured under guard by the richest men of the Orient. Why?

"Because"—he paused dramatically—"when swallowed as I have just swallowed the one you saw, the last one I own, they confer the priceless gift of prolonging life."

The boys listened with popping eyes. They could see that Mr. Won believed everything he said. Mr. Won drew a deep breath.

"This was discovered hundreds of years ago in China," he said. "The secret was kept by kings and nobles, later by wealthy businessmen such as myself. I am one hundred and seven years old because in my lifetime I have swallowed more than one hundred of the pearls of life, which the ignorant call Ghost Pearls."

He fixed his small, dark eyes now on Chang.

"You see, small dragon, why I must have the necklace at any cost. Each pearl prolongs life for about three months. There are forty-eight pearls in the necklace. To me they mean twelve more years of life. Twelve more years!"

His voice rose. "I must have the pearls. Nothing can stop me. You small ones are but dust in my path if you interfere! Twelve years of life—and I, one hundred and seven! Surely, small dragon, you see how important this is to me."

Chang bit his lips.

"He means it," he whispered to Pete and Bob. "He

won't stop at anything. I'll try to bargain with him."

"Bargain with me, by all means," said Mr. Won, who obviously had keen hearing. "That is the way of the Orient. An honorable bargain will be kept with honor on both sides."

"Will you pay my aunt for the pearls if Pete tells you where they are?" Chang asked.

Mr. Won shook his head.

"I have already said I will pay the man Jensen. I keep my word. But"—he paused, studying Chang—"there is a matter of difficulty with the mortgage payments on your honored aunt's vineyard and winery.

"It is I who own those mortgages. I give my word there will be no trouble. Your aunt shall have time to pay them. Also, the ghost who has terrorized the workers will vanish, and the workers will return."

All three boys blinked.

"Then you know whose ghost it is?" Chang cried. "How can you know that?"

Mr. Won smiled slightly.

"I have a large store of small wisdom," he said. "Lead Jensen to the pearls and your aunt's troubles will be over."

"That sounds good," Chang declared. "But how do we know we can trust you?"

Unconsciously, Pete and Bob nodded. That was the thought in their minds, too.

"I am Mr. Won," the old man said sharply. "My word is stronger than bands of steel."

"Ask him how we can trust Mr. Jensen!" Bob blurted out.

"Jensen would promise anything and do the opposite!" Pete chimed in.

Mr. Won raised his voice.

"Have the man Jensen sent to me," he said.

They all waited. For a long two minutes, nothing happened. Then the red door from the elevator opened and Jensen strode in. He came insolently toward Mr. Won and the boys, his dark features set in a scowl.

"Did you make them talk?" he growled.

"You do not speak to an equal!" Mr. Won said sharply. "You are a crawling thing of the night, fit only to be stepped on. Act like one!"

All three boys saw rage show on Jensen's face, then fear—deadly fear.

"Sorry, Mr. Won," he said in a choked voice. "I just wondered——"

"Be silent and listen. If these boys place the necklace in your hands tonight, you will see they are unharmed. You may tie them up, if necessary, so they will need an hour or so to get loose, but not too tightly. If they give you the necklace, any harm you do them you shall receive multiplied one hundred times. If you do not heed my warning you shall enjoy the Death of a Thousand Cuts."

Jensen swallowed several times before he could speak.

"Look," he said, humbly now, "all of Verdant Valley will be crawling with people looking for them. So far

I've managed to divert suspicion from Hashknife Canyon, where they left their horses. My men have reported it to be empty. But if I take them back there——"

"Perhaps you will not have to take them back there. Perhaps they can tell you where to find the necklace. I hope so. It will make things simpler."

Mr. Won rose. Standing up in his flowing robes, he was a very small man, hardly more than five feet tall.

"Come," he said. "They wish to talk this over among themselves. As it is a matter of life or death, they have the right to make a free decision."

They went from the room, Mr. Won taking slow, deliberate steps, and vanished behind a crimson hanging.

CHAPTER 14

A Fateful Decision

"Don't say anything you don't want heard," Chang whispered to the others as the two men vanished. "There may be a dozen ears listening. Let's talk a lot, kill time. Time is on our side."

"I'm glad something's on our side," Pete said gloomily. "Right now somebody else seems to have all the marbles. What I want to know is how you two got caught."

"I flashed my light around," Chang said, "and I got a glimpse of a man's face. I shouted to you, Pete. Then about five of them jumped us. They had us tied up and gagged in no time."

"Then they tried to fool you into coming after us," Bob put in. "Lucky you were smart enough not to fall for it. Jensen was really mad when you didn't come. He wanted someone to go through The Throat after you, but they were all big men and afraid to try."

"What I can't figure is how they came to be there," Pete said.

"Jensen said he got to the top of the rise just in time to see us turn the wrong way down Hashknife Canyon," Chang answered. "He boasted he was smarter than any kids, and guessed right away we'd try to make it home through the mines and aging caves. Somehow he knew all about the connection between the two valleys through The Throat. He went straight to the other end of it to wait for us. And he left several men in the cave in Hashknife Canyon to grab us if we came back that way."

Chang shook his head disgustedly. "I thought I was so smart!" he said. "And I just played right into his hands."

"It was only bad luck Jensen saw us before we were able to hide," Pete told him. "Anyway, now you know a lot of your workers were really working for Jensen, and that he's a crook. That certainly explains all the accidents and damage you told us about."

"Yes," Chang agreed. "Jensen and his men must have caused them. But I can't figure out why. It all started more than a year ago, when no one knew a thing about the Ghost Pearls."

"Well, anyway, after we were tied up," Bob said, "one of Jensen's men came rushing in to say we'd been missed and Chang's aunt had ordered the valley, the mines, everyplace searched for us. Jensen was fit to be tied himself.

But then he had an idea.

"We had come to a section where some old wine vats were stored, big ones. He put Chang and me into two wine vats and hammered them shut. Then they just put those vats on a cart, pulled them outside, and loaded them on a truck. I guess nobody thought it strange to see two wine vats loaded on a truck."

"It was a clever idea," Chang admitted. "Inside the vats we were helpless. I could even hear someone ask Jensen if he had seen us, and he said no, but that he was going to look in the pass that leads north from the valley to San Francisco. He said we'd been seen riding in that direction. He said he wouldn't come back until he'd found us. That gave him a very smart reason for being absent from the hunt, you see."

Pete nodded. Jensen might be a crook, but he certainly wasn't any fool.

"The truck took us several miles, I guess"—Bob took up the story again—"then stopped. The wine casks were unloaded and they let us out. We were in an awfully deserted spot."

"It was several miles up the pass leading to San Francisco," Chang interjected. "There was a station wagon waiting. Jensen put us into the station wagon in back, lying down with a blanket over us, and told the other men to hurry back and join the search, but to do everything to keep anybody from looking into Hashknife Canyon where we left the horses. And he told them that if

137

they caught you, Pete, they were to bring you and the pearls to a certain address in San Francisco."

"Well, they caught me, but they didn't get the pearls," Pete said with satisfaction.

"Jensen made that station wagon fly," Chang went on. "I guess we beat all records between Verdant Valley and San Francisco. When we got here, we drove into some kind of underground garage. Then some Chinese servants untied us, let us wash up, gave us a big meal, and that's the whole story until we were taken to talk to Mr. Won."

"I wish someone would give me a big meal," Pete groaned. "And let me wash up. Look at my hands! Well, my part of the story is that I heard you yell, and knew those flashes Jensen made were fakes. The only thing I could think of was to get out the way we came. I headed back. Lucky Bob had marked the trail in. That helped."

Bob held up his hand. Then, in the air with his finger, in such a way that their three bodies hid it, he made a "?," the mark of The Three Investigators.

"I also marked the cask I was in," he said, almost soundlessly. "I was able to get at my chalk. But who'll look inside one wine cask among thousands, and if they do, what will our mark tell them?"

"Even Jupe couldn't tell anything from that," Pete whispered back. "But we'd better talk normally or they'll think we are plotting something."

Chang pretended Pete had been about to tell them something important, putting on a little act for the benefit

138

of any unseen watchers.

"No, Pete!" he said loudly. "Don't tell us about the pearls. Just tell us how you got caught."

Pete told them his story. He knew Chang didn't want him to say anything about where the pearls really were— inside the skull of the burro—so he said he'd hidden the flashlight behind a rock and crawled out, only to be grabbed.

The men who grabbed him had twisted his arm, but when he told them the flashlight was back in the mine in a section they couldn't get to, they had blindfolded him, led him out of Hashknife Canyon to a waiting car, and driven him here to the same hiding place to which Jensen had brought the others. From their conversation he gathered that the search for all three was centering in the desert beyond Verdant Valley. Apparently the lies told by Jensen's men had kept anyone from finding the three horses in Hashknife Canyon.

Chang looked serious as he spoke.

"My aunt and Uncle Harold are probably frantic, looking for us," he said. "We can't hope to escape from Mr. Won. Whoever he is, he is a man of tremendous wealth and power and can do just about anything he wants. There's only one thing we can do. That's give him the pearls."

"You mean just hand them over?" Pete asked, thinking of all he had been through and the pains he had taken to hide the necklace.

139

"I trust Mr. Won," Chang said. "He has said we will be unharmed. He has said Aunt Lydia's difficulties will cease. I believe him."

"Do you suppose he really believes those pearls prolong his life?" Pete asked. "I mean, it sounds crazy."

"I'm sure he believes it," Chang answered. "It may even be so. It does not seem likely, but remember, the lore of China is centuries old. Only recently has western science found that the skin of a certain toad contains a valuable drug, yet this was known in China hundreds of years ago.

"And rich Chinese have always believed in the medicinal value of tiger whiskers and the ground-up bones of giants."

"I've read about that," Bob put in. "The giants' bones were really the bones of mammoths, from Siberia or someplace."

"So who can say if the gray pearls really prolong life?" Chang asked. "Mr. Won believes it, and sometimes belief alone is medicine strong enough to cure the ill or save the dying."

"I wonder just what he knows about the green ghost," Bob said aloud. "Funny, the way the ghost and the pearls both showed up at the same time and in the same place."

But Chang was not listening. He raised his voice.

"Mr. Won!" he said. "We have decided."

The draperies parted. Mr. Won came toward them. He was followed by Jensen, and three slippered servants.

"And your decision, small dragon?" Mr. Won asked. He had probably overheard everything they said, except the whispers, but Chang did not mention this.

"We will give Jensen the pearls to give to you," he said. "The pearls are back in the mine."

"Jensen can go to fetch them," Mr. Won purred. "You will remain my guests until then. Later you will be released. You do not know my name, or my whereabouts, and you are free to say anything you wish. If you are believed, none can find me. Even to the Chinatown of this modern day which exists around me, I am a mystery."

"It isn't that easy," Pete blurted out. "Jensen is too big to crawl through the spot where the roof has partly collapsed. Only a very thin man or a boy can get through!"

"I'll find a man——" Jensen began. Mr. Won clapped his hands in anger.

"No!" he said. "You must fetch them. We can trust no one. Let me question the boy. Look at me, boy!"

Pete found Mr. Won's small black eyes fixed on his. He couldn't have looked away if he wanted to.

"This is true?" Mr. Won asked. "Jensen cannot get through to the spot where you hid the pearls?"

"Yes, sir." Somehow Pete knew he couldn't lie. With Mr. Won looking at him that way his mind couldn't think of anything but the truth.

"The pearls were in an old flashlight?"

"Yes, sir."

"And you hid the flashlight. Where?"

141

"Under a rock."

"Where is this hiding place of the flashlight?"

"I can't describe it exactly," Pete said. "I can find it again, but I can't draw a map or anything."

"Ah." Mr. Won seemed to think. Then he spoke to Jensen. "The way is clear. You cannot send a man. Only the boy can find the flashlight. You must take him, he must regain the flashlight and the pearls, and give them to you. You will take all the boys."

"But the danger!" Jensen's swarthy face was sweating. "If they are searching in that canyon by now——"

"You must risk the danger. You must get the pearls. Then the boys go unharmed."

"But they'll talk! They'll have me arrested."

"I shall protect you. I shall pay you well and get you safely out of the country. They do not know the faces of yours assistants. So they can tell nothing damaging. As for me—no one can find me, and if anyone did, he could prove nothing against me. Do you understand?"

Jensen was breathing hard. "Yes, Mr. Won," he said at last. "I'll do it your way. But suppose they double-cross me? Suppose they don't give me the pearls?"

A long silence held the room. Then Mr. Won smiled.

"In that case," he said, "I am not interested. Dispose of them as you wish and make your way to safety as best you can. But I think they will try no tricks. They, too, love life, even as I do."

Bob felt himself shivering. He certainly hoped Pete

could find those pearls again.

As for Pete, he was thinking that actually Mr. Won had just asked him about the flashlight, and he had told the truth. It hadn't occurred to Mr. Won the pearls weren't in the flashlight any more. What good this would do, Pete couldn't see, but at least it meant he and Bob and Chang were being sent back to Verdant Valley, or anyway to Hashknife Canyon.

"Now haste," Mr. Won said. "It grows late."

"I'll tie them up and——" Jensen began.

"No!" Mr. Won said. "They will sleep until they reach the spot. Simpler, easier, and for them, more comfortable.

"Small dragon, look at me!"

Unwillingly, Chang looked into his eyes. Mr. Won stared at him fixedly.

"Small one, you are weary—very weary. You are longing for sleep. Sleep grips you in its soft arms. Your eyes close."

Bob and Pete, watching, saw Chang's eyes flutter shut for a moment. Then with an effort he opened them again.

"Your eyes close!" Mr. Won said again, softly, insistently. "You cannot resist me. My will is your will. Your eyes are heavy. They droop . . . they close . . . close tightly. . . ."

And indeed, now Chang's eyes did shut as if he could not control his eyelids. Mr. Won's voice continued its soft, insistent tone.

"Now you are sleepy," he said. "You are so very

143

sleepy. Sleep descends on you like a wave of darkness. You are sinking into sleep. Sleep overwhelms you. In a moment you will sleep, and stay asleep until you are told to awake. Sleep, small dragon . . . sleep . . . sleep . . . sleep . . . sleep. . . ."

His voice continued repeating the word until suddenly Chang went limp and toppled over, fast asleep indeed. One of the waiting servants deftly caught him as he fell, and carried him out. Chang did not waken.

"And now you, hider of my precious pearls. Look at me!"

It was Pete's turn now. He tried to avoid looking at Mr. Won, but Mr. Won's eyes drew his gaze as if they were magnets. Despite himself, Pete could not look away. Desperately he tried to fight the sleepiness that overwhelmed him as Mr. Won's whispered words went on and on, but in vain. Weariness such as he had never known before overcame him. After a few moments his eyes closed tightly and he, too, toppled into the arms of a waiting servant.

Bob realized Mr. Won was using hypnotism, which is often used to put people to sleep—in fact, he had read of its being used to make patients having an operation feel no pain. So he was not frightened when Won turned his gaze upon him.

"Smallest of all, yet stout of heart," Mr. Won said, "you, too, are weary. You would sleep like your friends. Sleep. . . ."

145

Bob closed his eyes. He toppled forward but was caught before he struck the floor. The third servant carried him out.

Mr. Won detained Jensen for one last word.

"It is well," he said. "They will all sleep soundly until you reach your destination. Then simply tell them to awaken, and they will wake. After that, the pearls—and the boys go free. Otherwise——"

He paused, then finished.

"Otherwise, you may slit their throats."

CHAPTER 15

Jupiter Finds a Clue

"But hasn't *anyone* seen any question marks?" Jupiter Jones asked in a baffled manner. He and Bob's father had just arrived at Verdant House in Verdant Valley after their hurried plane trip.

Miss Green shook her head. She seemed very weary.

"No one," she said. "I have the whole valley searching for any such marks. Even the children are being asked. No chalked question mark has been seen."

"What's all this fuss about question marks?" demanded Harold Carlson. His suit was wrinkled and he, too, looked very tired.

Jupiter explained that a question mark was the special symbol that he, Pete and Bob used to mark trails or to tell each other they had been at some spot. If Pete or Bob were free anywhere, they would leave a question mark, or even a trail of them, to mark their whereabouts.

"They rode through the pass, out into the desert, I'm sure," Harold Carlson said. "We'll find them tomorrow. I'm having an airplane search made as soon as it is light. If they were anywhere in or near Verdant Valley, their horses would have been found."

"Perhaps." Mr. Andrews, Bob's father, spoke now. His voice was grim. "Miss Green, Jupiter here has something to tell you, something he wants you to hear."

The woman and Harold Carlson waited. All four of them were sitting in the big living room of Verdant House.

"Miss Green," Jupiter said, making his round face look as adult as he could, "I like to try to figure things out and—well—I've been busy trying to figure out about the green ghost and that scream my partners heard. I figured out the scream didn't come from inside the house—it wouldn't have been heard. The house is too well built. I tested that. The scream had to come from outside the house.

"No ghost would have gone out in the garden to scream, would he, just supposing there are ghosts? So it had to be a living person. The people who were there that night weren't sure how many were in the party. Some said six and some said seven. I decided they were both right.

"Six men started into the house after the scream. The seventh man, the one who screamed, just stepped from behind some bushes and joined them. It was the easiest way to remain unnoticed. It's the only answer that fits the facts."

"The boy's right," Mr. Andrews said. "I can't imagine why Chief Reynolds and I didn't think of it."

Miss Green frowned. Harold Carlson looked impressed.

"It does sound logical," Mr. Carlson said, his brow wrinkled. "But why would anyone do such a thing? I mean, stand behind some bushes and scream?"

"To attract attention," Jupiter said. "A weird scream is a great attention-attracter. And it just happened there was a group of men coming up the driveway to hear it. Only it didn't just happen. Those men had been especially persuaded to go there. At least five of them had."

"Otherwise it would be entirely too much of a coincidence," said Mr. Andrews. "That becomes obvious when you think of it."

"There's just no other answer," Jupiter said. "Somebody walked through the development and suggested to different men he met that they go over and see the old Green mansion before it got torn down. He made it sound like a kind of adventure, so a little group joined him. Some of them didn't know each other so they didn't know he was a stranger.

"When his partner, hiding in the garden, saw them coming up the driveway, he screamed."

Mr. Carlson blinked at Jupiter, as if trying to understand. Miss Green looked puzzled.

"But—but why?" she asked. "Why should two men do

such a thing?"

"To get the group into the house." Mr. Andrews spoke now. "To get them inside so they would see the ghost and report it. I'm afraid it makes very good sense, Miss Green."

"Not to me it doesn't," Mr. Carlson objected. "To me it sounds like nonsense."

"Jupiter," said Mr. Andrews, "play the tape that Bob made that night."

Jupiter had the portable tape recorder ready. He pressed the *Play* button. A weird scream filled the room. Miss Green and Mr. Carlson jumped.

"That's just the beginning," Mr. Andrews said. "The recorder stayed on at full volume and picked up some of what the six men said. Tell me if you recognize any of the voices."

Jupiter let the tape run on. They heard the deep-voiced man speak, and Miss Green sat up, her eyes wide and horrified.

"That's enough," she said, and Jupiter turned off the recorder. The woman looked at Harold Carlson. "That was *your* voice, Harold!" she said. "You deepened it, the way you used to when you played villains in college plays. But I know it was yours!"

"After I played it a few times, I was pretty sure I recognized it," Jupiter said. "Not right at first. But the accent is similar to the way Mr. Carlson talked when we met him at the old house. For a disguise that night, he used a deep voice and wore a false moustache. In the

150

darkness that was all that was necessary."

Harold Carlson seemed to have collapsed like a bundle of old clothes.

"Aunt Lydia," he gasped, "I can explain."

"Can you?" Miss Green's voice was icy. "Then do so."

Harold Carlson gulped a few times, then started to talk.

The trouble had begun, he said, a year and a half before, when Chang had been discovered living in Hong Kong, and Lydia Green had brought him to America and announced that, since he was the great-grandson of Mathias Green, the vineyard and the winery really belonged to him and she was going to give them to him.

"But I always expected to inherit the property," Harold Carlson groaned. "After all, until Chang arrived, I was your only living relative, Aunt Lydia. And I worked hard here, building it up. Then I realized it was all about to be taken away from me!"

"Go on." Miss Green's voice was toneless.

"Well"—Harold Carlson mopped his forehead—"I conceived a plan. I would buy a lot of new machinery, borrow money from friends, put the place in debt, and have it foreclosed by my friends. I did that. I hired Jensen as an overseer and he brought some of his men along to help make trouble—damage equipment, spoil wine—things like that. Well, then you did something you had sworn you would never do. You agreed to sell the property down in Rocky Beach."

"Yes." Miss Green's voice was very low. "My mother

promised Mathias Green, before he died, that that property would never be sold even if it collapsed in ruins. But I—I was desperate. So I agreed to sell it. To pay the debts you incurred, Harold."

Jupiter listened with eager interest. He had figured out about the scream, and deduced that Harold Carlson was guilty in some way, but he hadn't been able to figure out why. Nor had he entirely figured out the ghost.

"I thought my plan to get the property away from you for the debts, and share it with my friends, was doomed," Harold Carlson said. "Then—then I received a message."

"A message?" Mr. Andrews spoke curtly. "What was it?"

"To go to San Francisco to see someone. I did. He was a very old man named Mr. Won. I was blindfolded, so I don't know where we met. He told me he had bought up the mortgages on the vineyard and winery, paying my friends a bonus to sell them to him and not tell me."

"But why should he do that?" Miss Green asked.

"I'm coming to that," Harold Carlson sighed. "He had something to tell me. There is a very old servant in his house who was a lady's maid for the wife of Mathias Green. She had been told by someone who read it in the papers that the old house was sold and would be torn down. So she revealed a secret she had kept for all these years.

"She told Mr. Won that Mathias Green's bride had been buried in the house, in a room later sealed up, and all the servants had been sworn to secrecy. But now the house

152

was being torn down, and she did not want the body of her young mistress of so long ago to be disturbed.

"Mr. Won also told me that the servant believed the young bride was buried with the famous string of Ghost Pearls around her neck."

Harold Carlson paused, mopping his face.

"Well, Mr. Won seemed to know everything. He knew I wanted this property. He knew the sale of that house would enable you, Aunt Lydia, to save it. So he had a plan for me.

"I was to make the house seem haunted. That might hold up the sale. At the same time it would give me a chance to search the house thoroughly, by myself. He told me just where the hidden room was. I was to break into it, get the pearls, then announce the discovery of the body of the wife, and say I really believed the house was haunted."

"Mr. Won seems to have thought of everything!" Bob's father commented grimly.

"He had it all worked out. I was to sell him the necklace for a hundred thousand dollars. I was to make sure a ghost was seen in the old house. Then when the ghost "came" to Verdant Valley, it would make the grape pickers here flee and ruin this year's wine production.

"This would bankrupt the winery. Won would foreclose the mortgage, and later on he would sell the business back to me for the hundred thousand dollars he gave me for the pearls. That way I would have the vineyard and winery and he would have the pearls, which for some reason he seemed terribly eager to obtain."

"Did he tell you how to fake the ghost?" Jupiter asked with keen interest.

"Yes. I'll come to that later. Anyway, the whole scheme as he outlined it seemed simple. I made my plans. I got Jensen all set to do the screaming. Then something we hadn't expected happened. The contractor started to tear down the house a whole week ahead of schedule.

"He'd already started wrecking it when I learned of it. I was frantic. I rushed to Rocky Beach with Jensen by a special plane, afraid the bride's skeleton would be found before I got there. Then the Ghost Pearls wouldn't be mine to sell. They'd belong to Aunt Lydia, and she would surely be able to pay the mortgage then.

"Well, I got to Rocky Beach before the wreckers had made much progress. When it got dark, I stationed Jensen in the bushes. Then I strolled through the neighboring development and I persuaded several men to come with me to the old house. Jensen screamed. We investigated. The ghost appeared.

"Some of the men informed the police. Jensen and I slipped away. He returned here to Verdant Valley, while I stayed in Rocky Beach. I slipped around town, making the ghost appear in a number of spots so the stories in the newspapers would be sensational and exciting.

"I didn't return here to Verdant Valley that night. I stayed in a motel under an assumed name, and next morning I rented a car and drove out to the mansion to search for the hidden room and the pearls.

"Unfortunately, the wreckers got a glimpse of the secret room from the outside and the chief of police had men guarding the house. I couldn't get in until you, Mr. Andrews, and the chief and the boys all arrived and we went in together.

"So when I did find the pearls, I couldn't quietly put them in my pocket without telling anyone and later sell them to Mr. Won. I returned here and received a telephone call from Mr. Won. He had read the stories and guessed my predicament. He told me to stage a fake robbery of the pearls."

Jupiter's round face bore a look of satisfaction.

"I figured you'd faked that robbery," he said. "As soon as I realized it was you making the ghost appear. After Bob spoke to me on the phone, telling me about Miss Green seeing the ghost and then about the pearls being stolen, it occurred to me that you were involved both times. You and Miss Green were alone upstairs when she saw the ghost, or whatever it was. If someone was making it appear, you had to be that someone. There wasn't any other possible suspect.

"And if you were making the ghost appear," Jupiter continued, while the others listened intently, "then whatever the scheme was, you were behind it and the theft of the pearls was part of it. Thus I deduced you faked the robbery. I thought Jensen might be in it with you, since you and he returned to the house together and he had plenty of time to tie you up before he went back to where he had left Bob and Pete and Chang."

"Yes," Harold Carlson admitted glumly. "I made the ghost appear in Aunt Lydia's room again to get the talk started once more. Then I took the pearls out of the safe to show them to the boys.

"It was all arranged for Jensen to rush in with news the ghost had been seen down in the vineyard. In fact, he had carefully rehearsed three men to pretend they saw it and spread the word, so that all of our pickers would be terrified and leave.

"I rushed out, leaving the safe unlocked. When Jensen and I came back alone, he tied me up and took the pearls. He was supposed to give them to me today, but he didn't."

Harold Carlson looked very indignant.

"He told me he was going to sell them to Mr. Won himself. He said I wouldn't dare complain because then my part in the scheme would come out. He's double-crossed me! He's been away almost all day. I suspect he's driven up to San Francisco with the pearls!"

"It's no more than you deserve, Harold." Miss Green's tone was sharp. "You certainly have been acting like a common criminal. But just now the pearls do not matter. We must find the boys. Where are Chang and Pete and Bob?"

Harold Carlson shook his head.

"I don't know."

Jupiter had a flash of inspiration.

"Maybe they suspected Jensen!" he exclaimed. "Maybe he grabbed them to keep them quiet!"

Bob's father nodded grimly. "That sounds to me like a very good theory," he said. "After all, Jensen is missing. You say he's been away almost all day."

"I can see how Jensen might hide three boys," Harold Carlson said. "But how could he hide their horses? I tell you, dozens of people have searched the entire valley and part of the desert beyond it."

"If only someone had spotted a question mark!" Jupiter said. "Bob and Pete would certainly mark their trail if they could."

They were all staring at each other when the door opened without a knock and the old servant, Li, bustled into the room.

"Sheriff here, missy," she said. "Sheriff have news."

"He's found the boys?" Miss Green cried, rising to her feet. But the grizzled, elderly man with a star on his faded blue shirt who followed Li in shook his head.

"No, ma'am," he said. "You offered a reward to anyone who found one of those question marks, and I got a kid here, named Dom, who says he saw one."

From behind the sheriff emerged a small, shy-looking boy in ragged overalls and shirt.

"Yesterday afternoon I see a mark like this." He traced a "?" in the air. "I do not know it mean anything. I go to bed. I wake up to hear my father and brothers talk about reward of feefty dollars Miss Green offer to first person who find

157

funny mark. I remember."

He looked hopefully at Miss Green.

"I get feefty dollars?" he asked.

"Yes, boy, yes!" the woman snapped. "If you're telling the truth. Where did you see this mark?"

"Inside a barrel. Out along the road in the desert," the boy said. "We all drive out to look in desert and I see barrel and I look inside. I see mark but nobody say anything about it yet so I do not know it means anything."

"In a barrel in the desert!" Mr. Andrews' voice sounded disappointed. "I can't see how that could be any help."

"I think we should go look at it, sir," Jupiter said, with restrained eagerness. "It could be important."

"I'm going with you!" Miss Green announced resolutely. "Li, get my coat."

"I'm going, too," Harold Carlson said.

"You will remain here!" the woman said firmly.

They all hurried out and climbed into the sheriff's old sedan. It took ten minutes to drive to the end of the valley and out into the desert beyond.

Several miles from the house, in a desolate section, their headlights showed two wine casks beside the road.

"There!" the boy Dom said, pointing. "First barrel!"

The sheriff played his light over the outside of the large casks, which stood upright. "Those are old, worn-out casks," Miss Green said. "They would never hold wine. I wonder what they are doing out here."

But Jupiter, Mr. Andrews and the sheriff were all trying

to peer into the cask to which Dom had pointed. They all saw clearly a wobbly question mark scrawled on the bottom of it.

Only Jupiter, however, realized it was in green chalk, and he knew what that meant.

"Bob was in that cask!" he said. "He left that mark for a clue!"

"Now I understand!" Miss Green cried. "Wine casks are such common objects, no one would notice two on a truck driving away. But they could have boys inside them!"

"By Jimminy!" the sheriff muttered. "Means they were nabbed, huh?"

"Probably taken out of the casks here and driven off!" Mr. Andrews said. "Very likely to San Francisco. And by that man Jensen, of course. It means we have to get the San Francisco police looking for him. Let's get back to the house and telephone."

They all re-entered the car and the sheriff backed it to make a wide turn. As he did so, in the headlights they saw a piece of paper fluttering beside the road, caught in a ball of tumbleweed. Only Jupiter sensed it could mean anything. At his insistence, they waited for him to climb out and get the piece of paper. He brought it back and they all examined it by flashlight.

"It's from a notebook," the sheriff said. "And there's writing on it."

"That's Bob's handwriting!" Mr. Andrews cried. "It

159

looks as if it were done in the dark, but I'd know it anywhere."

The note said, in very large, straggly letters:

39

MINE

HELP

? ? ?

"Thirty-nine—mine—help! And three question marks." Mr. Andrews frowned. Jupiter, however, had no trouble getting the general meaning of the note.

"Bob wrote that," he said tensely. "And he's telling us to look in a mine for him someplace."

"Well, mebbe," the sheriff agreed slowly. "But what's that thirty-nine? Thirty-nine miles?"

"I don't know what the thirty-nine means," Jupiter admitted.

"There is no mine thirty-nine miles away," Miss Green said. "All the mines are in Verdant Valley or in Hashknife Canyon. None of them has a number and I've been assured by the men that both the valley and Hashknife Canyon have been thoroughly explored."

They stared at each other, deeply puzzled and upset.

"Bob's note means he and Pete and Chang are someplace around here," Jupiter said slowly. "And they're in trouble. But how can we hope to locate them?"

CHAPTER 16

A Disastrous Discovery

Bob and Chang sat side by side with their backs against the wall of the cave that was the entrance into the mine where Pete had hidden the pearls. Very close on either side of them sat two men—Jensen's men—in case they tried to escape.

As their feet were tied together, there wasn't much chance of them going anyplace.

It was pitch dark and very late. They had lain under blankets in the back of a station wagon all the way back here to Hashknife Canyon. Then, when the car could go no further, they had been roused and forced to walk through the darkness here to the cave.

Pete and Jensen were now inside the mine, after the hidden pearls.

"Do you trust Mr. Won?" Bob asked. "Did he mean it when he said we'd be all right if he got the pearls?"

"I trust him." Chang's tone was thoughtful. "He is a very clever old man. He lives there in Chinatown in the old way, in secret, even though Chinatown itself has all changed and is really very American. I suspect most of his house is underground. And it may even be true that he is a hundred and seven years old.

"I saw how afraid Jensen was of him. I guess we're safe if Pete gives Jensen the pearls."

"But suppose Pete can't find them again?" Bob asked.

"Pete will find them," Chang said. "Pete is smart."

"I sure hope so," Bob answered, still in the same whispering voice so the two drowsy guards wouldn't shut them up. "You know, they put everything back in our pockets— my chalk, my notebook, pencils, knife, everything."

"That means they intend to set us free," Chang declared.

"Provided Pete can find the pearls again," Bob muttered. He remembered how much alike all the rocks inside the mine looked. It wouldn't surprise him a bit if Pete couldn't find the right rock again. He didn't know Pete had hidden the pearls inside the skull of the burro. That was Pete's secret.

Bob had an important secret of his own. He itched to tell it to Chang, but he didn't dare lest the two guards hear it.

They sat and waited. Only a mile or so away, in Verdant Valley, Jupiter and Miss Green and the others were desperately trying to figure out where to look for them, but without success.

They did not think of investigating Hashknife Canyon because it had been searched and found empty. However, it was Jensen's men who had "searched" it, and reported it empty, and Jensen was now deep inside the mine with Pete.

"You try any tricks on me, boy, and you're a gone gopher!" Jensen growled as their flashlights made crazy shadows along the narrow mine passages. "We have your horses penned in a little natural rock corral down by the waterhole at the end of Hashknife Canyon.

"If you don't come across with the pearls, all three of you go into that waterhole. It'll look like a terribly sad accident, and I'll be the saddest mourner of them all."

Pete shivered. He believed the big, burly man would do this. All he wanted was to get those pearls into Jensen's hands and have it over with.

"You kids!" Jensen snorted. "Thinking you could outsmart me! I figured out your trick of going through the mines the minute I saw you head down Hashknife Canyon the wrong way. I know all about these mine tunnels. When I move into a neighborhood, I always learn everything there is to know, just in case I have to make a fast getaway. I know every ridge and canyon for ten miles around here."

They came to the place where the collapse of the roof had squeezed the passage down to mere inches. Jensen gave Pete a last warning and Pete began to wriggle through on his stomach.

163

Having done it twice before, he was able to make good time. Soon he could stand erect again, and now he almost trotted through the mine galleries, following the trail of question marks Bob had left.

He came to the triple fork, took the right-hand passage, and was at the place where the skeleton of the burro lay before he realized what had happened.

Then, as he stood and stared, icy sweat broke out all over his body. The skull of the burro was gone!

Where it should have been was a rock as big as a wheelbarrow. A broken roof timber, and a gaping hole showed where the rock had plunged from the roof to fall on the white skull, crushing it into dust.

And the pearls had been inside the skull. They were delicate gems, easily crushed. Now they, too, were dust, mixed with the dust of the ancient bone.

CHAPTER 17

The Mysterious 39

Pete, when he could think, knew what had happened. He remembered that very faint tremor, that uneasy quiver of the ground caused by an earthquake someplace along the San Andreas fault line, which he had felt earlier that night when crawling out of the mine.

That echo of a distant earthquake had dropped the great rock on the Ghost Pearls and demolished them!

Now, no matter how much he wanted to, he couldn't give the pearls to Jensen.

Half-heartedly he tried to push the rock aside, but it was far too heavy. In any case, he knew it would be no use. There was rock under it, and when rock falls on rock, anything delicate in between is ground to bits.

Pete tried to think. It occurred to him he could keep

going until he reached The Throat. He could slide through The Throat and try to find his way out of the mines that way.

But once on the other side of The Throat, he had no idea of the way. He would probably get lost and might wander for days.

In any case, he couldn't save Bob and Chang that way. Long before he could hope to find his way out and get help, Jensen would realize he wasn't coming back, and take drastic action.

Then Pete remembered the flashlight he had hidden, with pebbles in it.

With the faint hope in his mind that he could use the flashlight to trick Jensen, he walked back down the passage. At the point where the three galleries all separated, he found the line of casually placed rocks that made a kind of arrow, pointing to a bigger rock.

Behind the big rock was the flashlight.

He wished now he had left the pearls in the flashlight. But the skull had seemed like a good idea at the time. Who could predict an earthquake?

He shoved the flashlight inside his belt and started back. He wasn't hurrying so fast now. He was trying to think of how to trick Jensen.

The only possibility was that Jensen would take the flashlight and not open it. On that Pete pinned his hopes.

He came to the low section and started to wriggle through it on his stomach. At the far end the man saw his flashlight beam moving and called to him.

"Hurry it up! I think you're stalling! You'd better get here fast!"

Pete kept crawling, his heart heavy. He wriggled out and stood up, brushing the dirt off himself. Jensen interrupted him.

"Give me that flashlight!" he growled. He saw the end of it and wrenched it from Pete's belt. He hefted it, felt the weight of the pebbles, and thrust it into his pocket.

"Now let's move!" he said. "I want to get out of here."

He started with long strides back toward the cave entrance. Pete hardly daring to hope, followed.

After about ten steps, Jensen stopped and whirled.

"How do I know you're not trying to put something over on me?" he growled, glaring at Pete. "I don't trust you kids. You're too big for your britches."

He jerked out the flashlight, twisted off the bottom cap, and poked a finger in.

As he did that, Pete's feet moved of their own accord.

He started running past Jensen, hoping to get beyond his reach.

As he went by, the burly man thrust out a foot and tripped him. Pete went sprawling headlong, lay for a moment dazed, then slowly and painfully picked himself up.

By now Jensen had found that the flashlight held only some pebbles wrapped in a handkerchief, and his fury was so great he could hardly speak. He growled some unintelligible words at Pete, then whipped out his knife.

Even by the light of a flashlight, the blade gleamed wickedly.

Jensen grabbed Pete's collar, planted the point of the knife against his back and said, "Walk!"

Pete walked, with the raging man behind him.

"You know what this means!" Jensen said, when his fury allowed him to talk intelligibly. "Mr. Won gave me the go-ahead if you tried any tricks. The sun will rise in a few hours now, but none of you will see it!"

Pete didn't even try to explain what had happened. Jensen wouldn't care. He was only interested in the fact he didn't have the pearls.

Presently they came out into the cave that was the entrance to the mine. Pete's flashlight picked out the dim figures of Bob and Chang, huddled against the wall, as if asleep.

Beside them were the figures of the two guards.

"On your feet!" Jensen barked. "We have to move fast —get rid of these nuisances and get out of here while we can!"

The two men stood up slowly. Then abruptly they had guns in their hands and Pete and Jensen were enveloped in the glow of half a dozen flashlights. Behind them barked the voice of Sheriff Bixby.

"Don't move, Jensen! You're covered from all sides!"

Jensen did move. He grabbed Pete, swung him around, and ran for the entrance dragging Pete behind him.

So sudden was his action, that no one had time to

tackle him. No one dared shoot for fear of hitting Pete.

At the mouth of the cave, Jensen let Pete go and plunged out, past two men who were standing there not expecting anything like this to happen. Almost flinging himself down the rocky canyon wall, Jensen was gone in the darkness before anyone could do more than fire a few aimless shots into the night.

"We'll get him tomorrow," Sheriff Bixby predicted. "By Jimminy, I'm glad to see these three sprouts safe and sound."

Pete, Bob, Chang, and Jupiter Jones, who had emerged from the rear of the cave with Sheriff Bixby's men, were staging a wild reunion, in the middle of which Pete thought to ask how they had got there. It was Mr. Andrews, his hand proudly on Bob's shoulder, who answered.

"Jupiter solved the mystery of the ghost," he said, "and after we found the mark Bob left in the wine cask, Jupiter also saw the message Bob had thrown out of the car telling us to look for you in a mine. We didn't have any idea what mine, but Miss Green remembered that you, Chang, used to explore these mines with an old prospector named Dan Duncan. He's sick in a nursing home up in San Francisco, but she telephoned him and he said that if we hadn't found you anyplace else, to look in the mine in Hashknife Canyon that has a cave for an entrance.

"He was sure that if we had looked in the other mines, and found nothing, this would be the one Chang might have headed for. The sheriff got some men and we slipped into the canyon, had a scuffle with the men guarding Bob and Chang—fortunately Jensen was too deep in the mine to hear it—and laid a trap for him when he came out."

Then he turned to Bob.

"Son," he said, "there's one question we'd like you to answer. Even Jupiter can't figure it out."

"Yes, Dad?" Bob asked.

Mr. Andrews looked at Jupiter Jones and nodded.

Jupe unfolded the note they had found, the note that said in large, ragged printed letters:

39

MINE

HELP

? ? ?

"Bob," he said, "we got all the message except the number. I suppose I should know, but—well, what does the thirty-nine stand for?"

Bob grinned. He brought out his notebook and opened it. It was just two covers now. All the pages had been torn out.

"Pete and Chang and I were all under blankets in the rear of a station wagon," he said. "Pete and Chang were asleep, but I was just pretending.

"When I figured we ought to be someplace near Verdant Valley, I slipped my notebook and pencil out and started writing messages for help. I had to do them in the dark, under a blanket, so I couldn't write much.

"As I finished each one, I slipped it out through a crack where the tail gate of the station wagon hinges to the rear. I hoped somebody would find one and be able to figure where we were. As I wrote out each one, I numbered it, so if anybody found more than one, he could tell he was following our trail in the right direction. That message was number thirty-nine. I guess the rest blew away."

Mr. Andrews started to laugh. The other men joined in. After the tension of the last few minutes, the mysterious thirty-nine and the simple answer to it seemed very funny.

Finally even Jupiter managed to grin. But it wasn't easy. After all, he was thinking, if he had realized the note was numbered, they could have looked hard for more notes and so found Bob's trail that way. He should have known Bob would be methodical. Wasn't Bob in charge of records and research for the firm?

But luckily the one note had done the job, after all.

CHAPTER 18

Jupiter Calls Up a Ghost

Jensen was not captured the next morning. Either he made good his escape, through his boasted knowledge of the territory, or he came to grief in some obscure canyon. In any case, he was never seen again. As for Harold Carlson, Miss Green, unwilling to prosecute a relative, sent him away with orders never to return.

Bob's father, with his son safe and a story to write for his paper, hurried back to Los Angeles. He exposed the green ghost as a hoax and told many of the details of what had happened, including the theft of the pearls and their destruction under a rock in the mine.

However, he played down the part of the boys in the adventure to spare them too much publicity, and he left out Mr. Won altogether, because he could learn nothing whatever about Mr. Won. Evidently the aged Chinese's boast that he had kept himself a mystery to the world was true.

Titus Jones phoned Jupiter that The Jones Salvage Yard could remain closed for a day or two, so Bob and Pete and Jupiter stayed on to enjoy a visit with Chang Green. Now that the ghost scare was over, the workers returned and the ripe grapes were picked and crushed on schedule. The boys had a good time with Chang, exploring the country, though Bob had to spend a couple of days resting because his leg was rather tired from the strenuous activity.

He spent his time writing up his notes of the case.

Jupiter wanted to see the mine tunnels, but when he saw The Throat and the low spot through which the others had crawled, he admitted it was just as well he hadn't been along. With his rotund, stocky build, he might have got stuck for good in either of the spots.

Eventually The Three Investigators returned to Rocky Beach. Soon after they arrived, Police Chief Reynolds took the trouble to see the boys personally and praise them for exposing the green ghost hoax.

. "I can't tell you how glad I am to know I wasn't seeing things," he admitted. "Any time I can give you boys a hand, call on me. Just to show you I mean it, here's a little something that might come in handy."

He handed each of them a small green card. Each card said:

This certifies that the bearer is a Volunteer Junior Assistant Deputy cooperating with the police force of Rocky Beach. Any assistance given him will be appreciated.

(Signed) Samuel Reynolds,
Chief of Police.

"Gosh!" Bob and Pete said. Jupiter turned pink with pleasure.

"Might come in handy sometime," the chief said. "Anyway, it'll show my men you aren't just snoopy kids if you start in doing something they think looks suspicious."

He left with their thanks ringing in his ears. The following day, when Bob's notes were completed, they went to call on Alfred Hitchcock, who took keen interest in all their cases since he had agreed to introduce them—if he thought they were well handled.

In the big office, the boys sat upright waiting while the famous motion picture and television producer read over the details of the case. From time to time he nodded and a couple of times he chuckled.

Finally he put the sheaf of papers down.

"Well done, lads," he said. "Quite an adventure."

"I'll buy a double helping of that!" Pete said fervently.

"The outline of the matter seems clear to me," Mr. Hitchcock told them. "Harold Carlson wanted to get the property for himself, so he borrowed money from friends, intending to see to it that the money was not repaid. In

175

this scheme Jensen aided him. Then Mr. Won, learning of the Ghost Pearls in the old house in Rocky Beach, bought the mortgage notes from Mr. Carlson's friends and applied pressure on Mr. Carlson to obtain the Ghost Pearls for him."

He leaned forward, tapping the papers.

"What of Mr. Won?" he asked. "He is a character who intrigues me. One hundred and seven years old, drinking pearls to stay alive, and living in the old style! Did you hear nothing more from him?"

They admitted they had. Bob told Mr. Hitchcock that a couple of days after his dad's story appeared in the newspaper, two small Chinese men had arrived in Verdant Valley. They came from Mr. Won. They wished permission to try to find the last of the crushed pearls under the rock that had smashed them. In return, Mr. Won would agree to give Miss Green as long as she needed to pay off the mortgage notes on the vineyard.

Miss Green had agreed. The two men had crawled into the mine with crowbars, and had come out bearing some kind of dust in a small leather bag. Whether it was pearl dust or bone dust, or what, no one knew. They went away without saying anything.

Mr. Hitchcock pursed his lips.

"I suppose," he said, "that the dust would do as well as the pearls themselves, if his men could actually recover it. Well, well, an interesting idea, that drinking dissolved Ghost Pearls can keep you alive. Perhaps mere superstition. Yet—perhaps not. We'll never know."

He fixed a keen eye on Jupiter Jones.

"Young Jones," he said, "though you were not along on most of the adventure, you seem to have been responsible for solving it. However, two questions nag at me."

"Yes, sir?" Jupiter asked politely.

"In these pages"—Mr. Hitchcock tapped Bob's notes— "I see a reference to the small dog one man carried into the Green mansion the night the ghost appeared. Apparently this dog helped you solve the mystery. What I wish to know is—how? What did that dog do that gave you any clues?"

"Well, Mr. Hitchcock," Jupiter told the director, "when I thought about that dog, I remembered a dog in one of the Sherlock Holmes stories. You'll remember that Sherlock Holmes told Dr. Watson to think about the curious incident of the dog in the nighttime."

"Of course!" Understanding spread over the man's features. "To which Dr. Watson replied that the dog did nothing in the nighttime. And Sherlock Holmes told him that that was the curious incident!"

"Yes, sir," Jupiter agreed.

Mr. Hitchcock leafed through the pages and found a spot. He reread it.

"That's it!" he exclaimed. "The dog which one of the men carried didn't do anything. He just whined a little, probably because he didn't like being carried. Young Jones, my hat is off to you for spotting that bit of evidence."

177

Pete and Bob were goggle-eyed. What could you tell from a dog that did nothing?

"I don't get it," Pete said. "So the dog didn't do anything. So what?"

"My dear young man," Alfred Hitchcock told him, "dogs and cats are universally considered to be very uneasy and frightened in the presence of the supernatural. Cats snarl and spit. Dogs howl and run. In any case, they kick up a fuss. So if this dog did nothing, it was because there was nothing there to frighten it.

"The deduction that follows is, whatever it was you and the men were seeing was not a real ghost, and so the dog paid no attention to it."

"Gosh!" Pete said. "That's right. And we missed that completely!"

"Never mind," Mr. Hitchcock told him. "You all behaved with great credit. You showed courage and determination, Pete. You, Bob, showed good sense in leaving clues that your friend Jupiter could find."

Mr. Hitchcock's brows creased slightly.

"Which reminds me," he said. "Mr. Won put you all three to sleep by hypnotism. Yet on the trip down from San Francisco, Bob, you were busy writing notes for help and slipping them out under the tailgate of the station wagon. Why were the others asleep, and not you?"

"I fooled Mr. Won." Bob grinned. "When I saw Chang and Pete topple over asleep, I knew what was coming. So as soon as Mr. Won started on me, I just toppled over as if

178

I'd gone to sleep instantly. Only I hadn't. I was awake all the time.

"That's how I was able to write the notes. Just about all of them blew away, though, in the desert wind. It was lucky one got caught in a tumbleweed so Jupe could find it."

"Luck," Mr. Hitchcock said, "has to be aided by ability. I feel all three of you showed great ability in this case. I will be happy to introduce it."

"Thank you, sir," Jupiter said, and they rose. They were almost out of the office when Mr. Hitchcock called to them.

"Wait!" he said. "I forgot the most important question of all."

He glared at them.

"Since there was no real ghost, what did all of you see?" he demanded. "Floating down hallways, disappearing through walls—what was it? And don't tell me it was cheese cloth covered with luminous paint because I know better."

"No, sir," Jupiter told him. "It was much cleverer than that. I didn't even suspect until I realized that the dog hadn't smelled anything or sensed anything so there couldn't really be anything there. May I darken your office?"

The director nodded. Jupiter closed the Venetian blinds and pulled shut the rich drapes that framed the windows. The office was now in a deep twilight.

"Watch on that wall," he said.

Mr. Hitchcock watched. Unexpectedly a greenish blob

of light appeared against the white wall. It looked like a ghostly Jupiter Jones in a white sheet. It glided slowly toward a closet door, then faded from sight as if melting away through the door.

"Amazing," Mr. Hitchcock said as Pete and Bob opened the curtains. "Under the right circumstances, that would be a very convincing ghost."

"With a weird scream and a haunted house to help along, it was too real for comfort," Pete declared. "Wasn't it, Bob?"

Bob agreed, as Mr. Hitchcock examined the object Jupiter handed him. It looked like a slightly oversized flashlight. But it had a special type of reflector and lens inside.

"It's really a miniature projector," Jupiter said. "It'll project a slide. But if you make the slide of a ghostly figure, out of focus, against a black background—well, when you project it on the wall of a haunted house, you get a mighty convincing ghost."

"And a beam of light could be made to glide slowly along a wall and up a flight of stairs," Mr. Hitchcock agreed. "Very ingenious. I judge that Mr. Won gave this to Mr. Carlson?"

"Yes, sir," Jupiter agreed. "When Mr. Carlson, wearing the false moustache and deepening his voice for a disguise, brought those men to the house to see the ghost, he just carried this in his hand. It looked like an ordinary flashlight to everybody.

"Some of the others had real flashlights, so they never noticed that this one didn't give off any light. Instead, Mr. Carlson used it to project the ghost image on the walls or the door. By turning a little button, he could make the image fade out as if it were melting through a wall.

"Up in Verdant Valley, when he took Miss Green up to her room, he just stood outside while she went into the dark room. He projected the ghost image into her room, from behind her, Then when she screamed and turned the light on, he just put the projector in his pocket, rushed in and caught her, and was rubbing her wrists when the others got there.

"It was a very convincing ghost, though, until I realized that somebody had to be at the Green mansion to do the screaming, that the little dog hadn't felt any supernatural presence, and that Mr. Carlson was alone with Miss Green when she saw the ghost, so he had to be the one really causing it."

Jupiter put the small projector back in his pocket.

"We're keeping this as a souvenir of the case," he said, and he and the others turned and filed out.

As he watched them go, a smile played around the director's lips. Sherlock Holmes himself might not have been able to solve the mystery of the green ghost any better!